Also by Jervey Tervalon . . .
Be sure to read his powerful national bestseller
DEAD ABOVE GROUND

"Hard to put down. . . . [Tervalon's] characters are so beauti-
fully drawn that readers will probably find them reappearing
long after the book is finished."
—*USA Today*

"Tragic, violent, but ultimately transcendent, *Dead Above
Ground* draws the reader in and never lets go."
—*The Times-Picayune* (New Orleans)

"A terrific read—scintillating and sultry, filled with murder,
mystery, and mayhem. *Dead Above Ground* is a blazing fever
of passion, vengeance, tears, and the ultimate triumph of a
woman's heart. Tervalon has woven magic."
—Jewell Parker Rhodes, author of *Douglass' Women* and *Voodoo Dreams*

"The city [of New Orleans] shimmers to life through the perfect pitch of the people who inhabit the tale."
—*Los Angeles Times*

"An arresting and profound literary experience. . . . An elec-
trifying novel. . . . Through these complex, superbly crafted
characters, Tervalon shows us that it is possible to be 'dead
above ground' in more ways than one might expect."
—*Gambit Weekly* (New Orleans)

Also by Jervey Tervalon

Living for the City

Understand This

Dead Above Ground

all the trouble you need

Jervey Tervalon

WASHINGTON SQUARE PRESS

New York   London   Toronto   Sydney   Singapore

A Washington Square Press Publication
1230 Avenue of the Americas, New York, NY 10020

Originally published in hardcover in 2002 by Atria Books

ISBN: 0-7434-2239-2

First Washington Square Press trade paperback printing February 2003

10 9 8 7 6 5 4 3 2 1

WASHINGTON SQUARE PRESS and colophon are registered trademarks of Simon & Schuster, Inc.

For information regarding special discounts for bulk purchases, please contact Simon & Schuster Special Sales at 1-800-456-6798 or business@simonandschuster.com

Printed in the U.S.A.

in memory of

LOUVERSA THIBODEAUX HARRIS

and

"PEPSI" (PECOLA TAYLOR)

acknowledgments

M uch thanks to the Nu Nu chapter of the Alpha Kappa Alpha Sorority, Inc., and to the Delta Sigma Theta Sorority at the University of California, Santa Barbara. I would also like to thank those beautiful book groups and their members who made *Dead Above Ground* such a success: Beverly Ware; Angela Harvey and her reading group; Marcia Sorey of Cover to Cover Book Club; Natalie I. Sanders; Wanda Poston of the Sister Circle Reading Group; L. Charmayne Mills Ealy's reading group; and Denise Dowdy of the Tabahani Book Circle; Linda Gueringer of Sassy Sistahs; Vivian Ewing of The Book Club.

Thanks, too, to those institutions that make this writer's life easier: Occidental College for the Remsen Bird Visiting

Acknowledgments

Artist position, and the Center for African American Studies at the University of California, Los Angeles. Thanks to PEN Oakland Center for the Josephine Miles Award and to the ever lovely Blanche Richardson at Marcus Books for the nomination. I very much enjoyed my afternoon at the Chester Himes Black Mystery Writers Conference and Award Program.

Also, thanks to the folks at Peet's Pasadena for my office away from home with all the good coffee, sweets, and a clean restroom this writer could need: Dylan, Zha Zha, Brendan, Leora, Anissa, Shaun, Jill, Nachi, Lisa, Scott, Andrew, Ryan, Mike, Paul, Oksana, Chris, Molly, Jen K., Jen H., Matt, Erica, Becky, and Tyson. And special thanks to Asha Parekh for her help with final-stretch revisions. And to my peeps: Eric "I Got Her Number" Chow, Jonathan "Cash Money" Gold, Tim "Philly Forever" Stiles, Lance "Married Bug" Kaplan, Cristian "How Late You Gonna Be?" Sierra, Bob "Hardest Working" Blaisdell, Marco "Nobody Gets Hurt" Villalobos, and Peter "Room Temp Cheese" Nye. And my man, Max Schott, for workshopping this a while ago. And my wonderful and beautiful cousin, Ellen Hazeur, who did so much for me in New Orleans!

And the biggest love for the girls: Gina, Giselle, and Elise.

—JERVEY

CHAPTER 1

City lights shot toward Jordan as he slammed on the brakes. He hit oil or water or something and slid out of the turn at the top of that steep hill on Carrillo doing fifty at least. Burning rubber and fishtailing, the back of the Triumph started coming around and for an ugly second he was sure he was dead, that the TR-6 would smack up against a curb, flip, and go bouncing down the hillside and explode like in some silly-assed action movie.

He got his wits about him, yanking his foot off the brake and steering out of the spin. The Triumph sputtered to the side of the road.

He sat there, engine idling, getting his head clear. Santa Barbara twinkled like colored glass below him.

It was a sign. He needed to turn around, go back home to

bed. No good would come of it, but he put the car into gear and continued on.

Jordan arrived, but he lingered behind the steering wheel, straining to see if he had the right house. Sometimes he parked a block away because all of the houses on Carrillo had high hedges or walls to ensure their privacy, but it also made finding the right address difficult, and when he did find the house it unnerved him to head down steep, narrow steps to the ornate wooden door that looked too much like the entrance to a tomb. Something seemed diabolical about that door and the Spanish-style house in general; it played on his secret fear that Mary might eventually get so mad at him she'd slip some arsenic in the wine, or a knife in the ribs.

Theirs wasn't a wholesome relationship; Jordan regretted it for many reasons, but even more so now that he was interested in Trisha. He rang the bell half hoping Mary had given up on him and had gone to sleep. He turned to leave.

Too late—he heard quick steps; the door opened and there was Mary smirking at him in a tight black slip that revealed her ample cleavage to its best advantage; but it wasn't her breasts he paid attention to, it was that smirk. Mary wasn't a bad-looking woman—she had a nice shape and a pretty enough face—but that damn smirk drove him nuts.

"Why are you so late?"

"I'm late?"

"Two hours late!"

"Two hours? How do you figure?"

"Ten, that's when you said you'd be here."

"You want me to leave?"

She paused to consider his offer, fingers twisting her thick brown hair as she thought it over.

"Yeah, go home. I don't need the aggravation."

"Neither do I," Jordan said, turning to head back up the stairs, but before his foot touched the first step Mary jerked him into the house.

"You asshole! You're staying. I didn't wait all this time for you to walk out!"

She pushed Jordan ahead of her through the dark hallway, almost causing him to fall flat on his face.

"Serves you right," she muttered from behind him.

She rented a room on the ocean side, from the weird-ass owner. Jordan had only seen him a few times but that was enough. So blond he looked bleached of color, dressed like a shaman, leading a workshop of loser New Agers, burning incense, chanting endlessly and purifying themselves by night swims in the frigid ocean water, all of that going on below the bluffs while he and Mary were angrily screwing their brains out.

Mary pushed him once more into her bedroom and onto her big bed.

"Get undressed!" she said.

"I'm leaving my shoes on," he said, to piss her off.

"Not on my bed," she said, and slid on top of him before he could unbuckle his pants.

"So what's it gonna be, a dry hump?" she asked.

That did it. Whatever self-consciousness he felt with her was gone. She got his fly open and before he could rip open a condom she tossed it aside and worked him in.

"I'm back on the pill; you don't need that."

3

He didn't feel right barebacking, but he gave in without much of a fight.

"Put your hands on my ass!"

"No, your tits," he said.

He held her breasts, but she pulled his hands off and forced them to her cheeks.

"Grab my ass!"

He did, hard; wanting to squeeze her cheeks until she stopped with the smirk.

"Oh, yeah! That's the trick!" she shouted.

He wasn't giving in.

She couldn't make him come. Not this sex-crazed white girl. She didn't have the power.

"Do it!" she shouted.

He came so hard it hurt. As fast as he came he wanted to go, go so fast she wouldn't notice he was gone until she heard the roar of the Triumph burning out.

She rolled off him, sighing and rubbing herself.

"Man, you pounded me. Guess you couldn't find someone to give it to, horny bastard."

"Yeah," he said, feeling that if she said another word he'd jump right out of his skin.

"You're not going to start with that post-fucking depression. That I don't understand. Why can't you enjoy yourself without making everything such an issue? It's just sex."

"I'm not depressed."

Suddenly modest she pulled the sheet over her breasts and propped herself up with a pillow and stared at him.

"Why are you covering your eyes like you're facing a firing squad?"

"I'm thinking."

"You better not be thinking about leaving. You leave, that's the last time you leave. You don't fuck and leave."

"That's not what I'm thinking."

"What are you thinking?"

She was right. He wanted to leave more than anything he had ever wanted in his life.

"Mary, I got to go. I have to prepare for my class tomorrow."

She began to cry.

"I'm not going to argue. I'm not going to get mad at you. But you know you can throw everything we have away if you walk out on me."

God, he wanted to go.

"Why don't you face it? You're scared to admit we have a relationship. So, you run."

"What are you talking about?"

"You don't want to admit you have feelings for me."

"I admit that. I have feelings for you."

"But you're not serious."

"I can't be serious. I explained that."

"What, that you can't be serious about a white girl?"

He couldn't bring himself to respond. Instead he pulled the pillow over his head and unexpectedly started to drift off.

He woke later that night feeling her ass pressed against his crotch, grinding slowly, so slowly he suspected she might be sleeping and the grind was a horny reflex. He twisted a bit until he was inside of her. He did her slowly, hoping, fantasizing that she'd sleep through it and he wouldn't have to listen to her rant about their relationship. The women he had the best sex with were the ones he wanted to run the fastest from. He was doing her comfortably and effortlessly, rapturous without the effort. No weight of responsibility, just the pleasure of luxurious carnality, but at the peak of the pleasure curve he thought of Trisha and her virginity; twenty-one and still a virgin.

How did that happen?

Christian family? The isolation of being a black girl in a very white world? The idea of her having that kind of restraint appealed to him, not because she was fresh or he'd be the first. It was that he imagined she had to be more uncomfortable about her sexuality than he was self-conscious about his own. They'd be perfect together. It had to be better than sleeping with people who make your stomach churn.

Fully awake, Mary slammed into him harder and harder, a piston of passion.

It was almost like magic; as soon as he came, the feeling of being trapped like a rat returned.

"Did you like that . . . ?" she whispered, turning her head for him to kiss her.

"It was great. . . ."

"Every night. You can come over every night and have me all you want."

"That sounds great," he said, without conviction.

A long moment passed.

"Are you still seeing that sorority girl?"

Jordan had forgotten he had mentioned Trisha to her.

"I'm not seeing her the way you think."

"What . . . you're not fucking her?"

"She's a virgin."

"Oh, a challenge?"

"It's not like that," he said, regretting ever mentioning Trisha to Mary.

"You think this Trisha is it, don't you?"

"I didn't say that."

"An African American girl from Santa Barbara; she probably comes from a family with a little money. You must think you've hit the jackpot."

Jordan rushed out of bed and dressed so fast he had to stick his boxers into his pocket.

"Yeah, I know. This is it," Jordan said, slamming the door on his way out. Mary talking to him about Trisha got him feeling more the self-loathing dog than he thought possible.

He drove home, racing over the seaside hills more relieved with each mile he put between them.

He opened the door of the dumpy duplex on Milpas and took four or five steps into the dark living room, kicked something soft, and sprawled face-first onto the dirty carpet.

"Oh, man!" he heard a voice say, and a big burst of a gasp. A light came on and there was Ned, his housemate in his boxers, laughing at Jordan and the crumpled man at his feet. It was a very confused Arturo. Jordan helped him up off the floor.

"Sleeping in front of the door? What's up with that?"

Arturo checked himself over, dusting off his suit. He seemed to always buy the same sharkskin suit, narrow lapels and cuffs, a kind of *Man from Uncle*, sixties, secret-agent thing.

"I was pretty buzzed. Next to the door seemed like a good idea."

"Yeah, he's been downing mixed drinks at an art opening," Ned said.

"Miko was there."

"Miko? She's still torturing you?"

"Oh, man, you don't know. Now she's going out with some dumb-ass surfer painter who cleans hot tubs."

"Nothing lower than a hot-tub cleaner," Jordan said, with a straight face. He had to clean hot tubs just last quarter when a course he was supposed to teach was canceled.

"He picked a fight with this big doofus," Ned added.

"He thought I was some kind of punk!"

8

"Yeah, he threw you into a hedge."

"Ned had to hold me back."

"Yeah, the next time he threw you over the hedge. Art tells me he's gonna say hi to Miko, next thing I know it's like Daffy Duck charging this big beef-eating white boy. Art's got a lot of heart. He stood up to him and got thrown about ten feet."

Art slumped onto the couch, already starting to nod.

"That's what happened. This stupid couch hurts my back," he said, sliding to the floor again.

"What hurt your back is getting tossed like a beach ball."

"I made my point."

"What's that? You can take a licking and keep on ticking?"

"You nitwits leave me be. I need my sleep."

Ned laughed and headed back to his bedroom.

"I wouldn't have missed that for the world," he said, and shut the door.

Jordan turned to leave but Arturo called to him.

"Hey, you have a spare blanket?"

Jordan nodded and pointed to the sleeping bag on the far end of the couch.

"Oh, yeah. Ned put that out there for me. I thought it was a pillow."

Jordan turned off the light.

"Hey, Jordan, I never see you lovesick. What's your secret? 'Cause I hate living like this."

"It's all about controlling your emotions," he said, as though he knew what he was talking about. If Art was asking him for advice, he must be really fucked up.

"Did it work with that Jamaican girl? Didn't she borrow your credit card to get a plane ticket to visit her man in New York?"

"Yeah, I almost forgot about that."

"And didn't she hit you in the head with a trash can in the lunchroom of the college?"

"Yeah, but that was a plastic trash can, not one of those metal ones."

"Yeah, and what about her posing nude for an art studio after you asked her not to, then she got down with the instructor?"

"Okay, what's your point?"

"'Least you were smart enough to get away from her. Me, I still hang around like a sad dog trying to get Miko to come back to me, but she likes messing with my mind. She even tells me how surfer boy likes to have sex with her."

"She told you that?"

"He's an anal man."

"She's into that?"

9

As soon as Jordan asked the question he felt like he was taking advantage of Art. If Art was sober Jordan wouldn't be asking him about the love of his life's sexual likes and dislikes.

"She says she just screams."

"She shouldn't be telling you that kind of shit."

"She says her screams get him excited. She likes that, gets her off."

Jordan heard Art sobbing like a little kid in the darkness. "Art, I got a half of a fifth of Jack Daniel's."

"Great," Art managed to say between sniffles.

Jordan found the dust-covered bottle on the bookcase without having to turn the light on, but he almost kicked Art again handing it to him.

"You want a cup with some ice?"

"No, it's more pitiful this way. Down on my luck, drinking stale whiskey, crashed out on a dirty carpet, wondering why the world is so down on the Mexican."

"That's pretty pitiful."

"Thanks, Jordan, you're a real pal."

"Don't mention it."

"How's that cutie pie Trisha treating you?"

"We're doing okay."

"Oh man, she's fresh to the game. You can shape her the way you like."

"You sound like a pimp."

"Yeah, being a loser at love makes you bitter."

"'Night, Art."

"'Night, Jordan."

*   *   *

Jordan woke to a knock.

"Hey, J—get dressed. We've got to make a run," Ned yelled through the door.

"It's eight in the morning."

"It's an emergency."

Jordan put on his pants and opened the door. Ned looked more irritated than Jordan felt; early light meant a lot to him. Every morning Ned painted landscapes on the north campus, and he had on his artist uniform, paint-stained sweatshirt and jeans.

"It's sick. Phil lost a finger at the Art Co-op in Summerland."

"That's messed up, but what are we supposed to do about it?"

"Art wants us to go with him to find it."

"Don't paramedics do that?" Jordan asked.

"Not unless you pay extra."

Soon they all crowded into Art's VW Bug and started south on Milpas.

"Your cat ate the finger?" Jordan asked.

"Not my cat. It could be any cat. They have lots of cats out there. My cat doesn't fuck with raw food," Art replied.

"But it could have been your cat. Maybe those other cats are messing with her mind. Your cat's probably gnawing on a knuckle as we speak," Ned said.

A mile from the freeway Art abruptly turned into the drive-through of a Jack in the Box.

"I need a big cup of ice and a breakfast burrito," Art said to the Jack. "You guys want anything?"

"You got a strong stomach," Ned said, "but I'll take a coffee."

"Me too," Jordan added. "But do we have time for this?"

"You have to make time for breakfast," Art said.

Ned coasted off the freeway, exiting toward the ocean south of Santa Barbara. Summerland, as sun-washed and ocean-cooled as the prettiest beach towns along the coast, had a reputation for being a very haunted town, and rumors of a half-dozen covens, headless horsemen, and haunted restaurants enhanced that reputation. What attracted Ned and Art and fired them up like Summerland was heaven was the offer of subsidized art studios. "Converted barns, plenty of loft space!" was the selling point, the economy of living above one's work like a dime-store owner. Art unlocked a barn door, pulled the wide door open, and they stepped inside. Once there, Ned and Jordan shrugged, reluctant to start the search for the bloody finger.

"I'm checking the table saw. Phil found two, but the index finger's missing. We're supposed to put it on ice," Art said, as he held up the huge soft-drink cup.

"So that's why we stopped," Ned said.

"Just doing my duty," Art said, and went off to the table saw.

Ned and Jordan sipped coffee and wandered about, looking over the cluttered, sawdust-covered floor, nudging around in a desultory search.

Art returned, chewing some ice from the Big Gulp cup.

"See anything?" he asked.

"No."

"The table saw was finger free. Phil might be out of luck."

All three of them focused on a cat walking on the paintings stacked along the wall.

"What's it got in its mouth?" Ned asked.

"I don't see anything in its mouth," Jordan replied.

Art flung some ice and the cat disappeared behind racks of draped, dust-covered paintings. They headed toward the rear of the barn studio near the kitchen where the clutter was more mazelike.

"Hey, Art, is that yours?" Jordan asked, pointing to a long horizontal oil of a brown man in peasant white slumped onto the back of a galloping horse.

"Just finished that one. That's my great-great-grandfather escaping from Mexico. He got shot in the Revolution."

"A war hero," Jordan said.

Art shrugged. "He fought on the wrong side. He headed north and stayed."

Art led them to the blood-stained table saw.

"Maybe we should look around here again," Art said, and he and Ned began an earnest search at the base of the table saw.

Jordan knelt and sifted through the sawdust; hoping for failure, he made another halfhearted attempt. This time he touched the finger. Jordan shot up, backpedaling into a rack of paintings. Calming himself he returned and bent to pick it up. He hoped that maybe it had slithered away. But there it was, waiting on him to get around to wrapping it up in the ball of tissue paper in his hand. To get on with it, like he needed to get on with everything else. The bloody little stub of a finger seemed to wiggle as he picked it up.

"Ice! Where's the damn ice!" he shouted.

Later at the hospital, a nurse ran with the finger like it was about to explode. They waited like expectant fathers for word on the fate of the finger.

"Glad it was you who found it. Phil's cool and all, but finding body parts . . . I'm not with that," Ned said.

"I didn't want to find it. It touched me."

"Touched you? Stop lying," Ned said. "What else is it going to do? It's just a finger."

"I think Jordan's right. It's Summerland. The place is haunted. That finger is too," Art said, and left to see how the operation was going.

Ned and Jordan watched the crowd grow in the emergency waiting room as the morning passed, teenagers waiting for treatment clutched broken arms from skateboard splats and bike accidents.

"How's Phil paying for this? Does he have insurance?" Jordan asked.

"Naw, he's broker than me. What artist has insurance?" Ned asked.

"I teach and don't have it," Jordan replied.

"That's why I'm leaving. I can't live like this forever. I love it and all but sooner or later you need more, like a job with health care and a house with a water heater that gives more than ten minutes of hot water. I need a sister to be down with. If I stay here cutting shrubs and working on rich white folks' estates I might as well be a bagman, put all my stuff in a shopping cart with my art degree, and find some hole in the ground to live in," Ned said.

"That sounds like a plan. Why didn't you think of it before?"

"Jordan, don't be an asshole."

"You're gonna miss it when you're gone."

"You just don't want to be the only Negro hanging out at the cafés scamming white chicks," Ned said, laughing.

"It's not as simple as that. It's hard to find many black women here. Plus, all the brothers are chasing them anyway."

"That's why you got to get hooked up with Trisha. She'll straighten you out. Settle you down."

"Yeah, that's just what I need. Settle down right now and sprout some roots," Jordan said, sarcastically.

"You can't be an exile from black life forever. This is a good life if you don't want more than beautiful mountains and the ocean," Ned said.

"Listen, wherever I live there's gonna be black life because I'm black and I've got life. Unless I'm mistaken and somehow I've become a dead white man and didn't notice it. People move around; Mexicans live in Chicago, Jews live in Utah. Why can't black people live in Santa Barbara?"

"Watch, when I come back to visit, you'll be tanning and surfing and eating bean sprouts," Ned said.

Art returned, smiling.

"All the fingers are back on. He can blow his nose or beat off with either hand."

"Aw, Art, you sick," Ned said. "Art, you still need a place to stay?"

"Yeah, I can't keep crashing on your couch."

"Here's your new roommate," Ned said, pointing to Art. "Art, try to act black for him so he knows what he's missing."

"Act black? It's hard enough being Mexican. Everybody thinks I'm a waiter."

"Maybe it's the suit. Either a waiter or a mortician," Ned said.

"Do I get a break on the rent? I'll be soul brother number one."

CHAPTER 2

"Now, this is the promised land. Once you've seen Santa Barbara, you can't go home again. Nothing compares," Benito said, with much sincerity.

Jordan wanted to nod yes, but his head was stuck in the washbasin as Benito scrubbed his soapy scalp. He was surprised that Benito brought up love of Santa Barbara, but maybe being the only decent black hairstylist in town he was doing so well he had to shout it out. Jordan didn't feel comfortable with that; it was like admitting you wanted to be surrounded by white people for the rest of your life outnumbered three hundred to one. How could any self-respecting black man be comfortable in that situation? Jordan was, and he wanted to stay in this picture-postcard world, even if it made him feel guilty. Life was a permanent vacation; a swim in the ocean, a hike in the hills, coffee in the morning at the Café

Roma, teach a composition class in the afternoon. He imagined himself living like that for the rest of his life; all he needed was a condo near the beach, and he was willing to give up a kidney, maybe even throw in a lung to get it. Property was the impossible dream of folks starting out in Santa Barbara.

"You're from L.A.?" Benito asked.

"Yeah, the Crenshaw area," Jordan replied.

"You like living there?"

"Oh, yeah. I try to get back as much as I can. I damn sure miss Roscoe's House of Chicken and Waffles," Jordan said.

"Really? Sounds to me like you lying," Benito said, in his coolish, quiet storm voice.

Suddenly uncomfortable, Jordan laughed nervously, trying to keep the shampoo out of his eyes.

"I'm not lying. I grew up in L.A. My family is down there. When I finish my thesis I'll move back to the real world."

Benito finished rinsing his scalp, "Oh, don't take me serious. I'm just clowning you. See, I don't have a problem living somewhere pretty, where the sunsets are gorgeous and I can see mountains out of my back window and the ocean out of my front door. It's a wonderful life. Plus, well, I can't lie. I don't have problems with blonds. I like them; I like them surfers."

"Surfers?"

"Yeah, my husband's up before dawn looking for waves."

Strangely, Jordan didn't feel uncomfortable learning about Benito's love life. He never easily admitted to dating someone white; maybe it was different if you were gay, different rules. He just told the truth about himself. Jordan wondered about that; telling the truth about himself wasn't something he easily did.

Later, after Benito was finished with him and as Jordan

was readying to leave, he saw a familar SUV park in front of the small salon. An attractive young black woman got out; it was Trisha and then her mother, Lady Bell. Trisha was dressed in slightly baggy jeans and a fashionably short blouse. She wore her hair pulled back in a hasty, ready-for-the-beautician bun. Her very short and attractive mother wore a beautiful Spanish-style skirt and boots; her long pepper gray hair trailed down her back, and the red blouse she wore made her dark skin even more vibrant. A very attractive woman in her late fifties, Lady Bell lived her life with such joy that it was heady just being around her. Jordan was hopelessly charmed by her, as everyone was. Benito turned from Jordan and rushed to open the screen door for them.

"Lady Bell! So good to see you and your lovely daughter." He had this suddenly odd accent that seemed slightly Germanic.

Lady Bell pulled him down a bit so she could kiss his cheek, and of course Benito beamed. Trisha smiled at Jordan, shrugging with embarrassment; then Lady Bell noticed him.

"Jordan!" she said, and still holding Benito's hand, kissed Jordan on the cheek. Lady Bell made effusive cheek, kissing seem a natural and comfortable act.

"When are you coming to dinner again?" she asked.

"Oh, as soon as Trisha invites me."

"Well, I've got the jump on her. I'm inviting you this Sunday," she said.

Jordan nodded.

"I have two open chairs. I can do you both at once," Benito said, as he rushed them to the washbasins. Trisha gestured for Jordan to call, and he nodded. He liked Trisha a lot, but she wore that plain gold cross for a reason. Jordan was devoutly agnostic, more pragmatic than spiritual. He knew that anything happening with Trisha would require serious commitment.

Outside, it was another gorgeous afternoon; the ocean glittered not two miles from where he stood, and the cloud-capped mountains were even closer. He loved speeding along the 101 on days like this, cranking Al Green to the top of the Triumph's speakers. Driving made him happy, sometimes too happy, but he paid the tickets and tried to love it a little less. The ragtop had to come down, even though it would be a bitch to get it back up when the ocean chill blew in later. He had just about got the latches open and the frame folded correctly so that it wouldn't rip another hole into the canvas of the ragtop when Trisha came out of the salon with her hair wet, a smock over her blouse and jeans.

"What time are you picking me up tonight?"

"Tonight?"

"Tonight's the AKA dance."

"I forgot all about it."

"You said you'd go."

"Yeah, now I remember."

"You should. You said you were looking forward to it."

She was doing it again. That weapon of hers, looking down at her feet and transforming into a very young girl whose fragile feelings were his to destroy.

"I don't remember, but I'll go," he said.

It worked. She smiled and kissed him just hard enough to make him think it would be worthwhile putting up with the embarrassment of being revealed as a stiff-ass dancer. Last time he went clubbing, a Latina had told him he danced like he was constipated.

"I'll see you at seven. You can help us set up the refreshments," she said, and returned to the salon.

He watched her walk back into the salon, thinking how much he liked her. It was surprising to him that he did; he had never been attracted to someone as conservative, or as practical, someone who wanted to go to law school. They were very different. All he wanted was more of the same, for very little to change. He liked life the way it was.

Ned was stretched out on the sofa showing the effects of clearing brush high up in petrifyingly beautiful Santa Ynez, at an estate close to where Michael Jackson had built his Neverland Ranch. Faint white tracks of dried sweat lined his dark forehead, his jeans and sweatshirt were dotted with thistles, and the boy was out cold, water jug resting on his stomach. Ned worked hard for the money, scuffling to pay his share of the tourist-town rent by doing all the shit jobs he could find, and he had the extra burden of needing studio space to do his art. He and his artist friends had a network of rich white folks to work for; some who even paid fifteen dollars an hour for back-breaking labor, and that was great for Santa Barbara, where you better be born with money because it was too damn hard to earn much of it.

"Wake your dead-ass up!" Jordan shouted.

Ned bolted, spilling the water jug across his chest.

"Goddamn!" he yelled.

The jug bounced off him and onto the shitty shag carpet.

"You dog!" he said, throwing the plastic jug at Jordan.

"You feel up to a dance tonight?" Jordan asked.

Ned didn't answer because he was twisting out of the

soaked sweatshirt. Even in the late afternoon sun it was easy to see the welts rising across his chest and stomach. Jordan remembered the one and only time he had tried to clear brush, and the resulting lacerations and that encounter with poison oak were enough to keep him down in the city.

"Jordan, be for real. Look at me. I slipped down a hill and bounced my ass all the way to a retaining wall. Almost broke my ribs. Man, I hate these rich bitches and their stupid estates."

"Gonna be refreshments . . ."

"Refreshments?"

"And it's an AKA dance."

"That's your new girlfriend's sorority?"

"Yeah, she's the president. Gonna be lots of sisters there."

Ned smiled. He wouldn't get involved with white girls, even though that was about the only way he'd get near getting some. He was devoted fully and hopelessly to black women, but unfortunately most black women at UCSB weren't interested in black men who walked around in paint-stained jeans and drove a beat-up VW van and had to clear brush to afford cadmium red and cobalt blue oils and plenty of canvas and stretcher bars.

"I don't know. What am I going to wear? You know I'm not a pimp like you."

"Borrow one of my jackets."

"Yeah, maybe," he said, but Jordan knew that tone. He was probably going to drive to his unheated little studio on the mesa and spend the night trying to keep his hands warm enough to paint.

"What do you think of virgins?" Jordan suddenly asked.

"Virgins? You know a virgin?"

"Yeah, I do. There's going to be one at the dance."

Ned rubbed his hands together.

"It depends. You interested?"

"I don't want to be. Virgins scare the hell out of me; all of that responsibility. Then you've got to ask yourself, why is she still a virgin at twenty-three?"

"Who is she? A freak white chick who wants to have her cherry stolen by a strong black brother?"

"Naw, it's Trisha."

"Trisha? She's a virgin? You need to marry her, and you said her family's got money. You'd never have to leave Santa Barbara. It's your dream come true."

"Yeah, I guess you right," Jordan said. "That's what it would mean. You know, it's right there. She doesn't even have to say it. If I hit it, it's forever. It's scary."

"What if you just hit and run?"

"I don't know if I could stand the guilt."

"She's got you feeling guilty and you haven't even done nothing. She's good."

"Yeah, she's real good."

"You know you gonna get married, might as well marry money."

"I think in your case, being one broke-ass painter, that's advice you should be considering."

Ned hurled his boot at Jordan's head.

He had only been to her family's house once before. They lived in the San Antonio Creek Road area in a development of mini-mansions in the foothills above the city. That first visit he wondered if the clutch on his '72 Triumph would make it up the increasingly steep roads and then the sharply angled driveway to her house, but it did, and he marveled at the view they had. The city unfurled gorgeously below. He could see all the way to the ocean and the Channel Islands at the horizon. The expensive view was at least $950,000 worth. He spent too much time depressing himself keeping up with the ridiculous prices of dot-com, entertainment-inflated Santa Barbara real estate. He and Ned could barely afford the thousand-dollar-a-month rent on their hovel-like house on Milpas. Teaching at the university sounded good, but it was a mug's game; the state paid in pinto beans and tortillas.

He didn't think he was that late. What, twenty minutes, but there she was in the doorway, arms folded, in a bright pink jacket and skirt with a green blouse; maybe if she had some pink go-go boots it would work.

"Nice outfit," he said.

"Don't try to flatter me. I know this thing is ugly, but I'm an AKA sorority president. I'm expected to wear the colors."

Jordan shrugged. Trisha didn't try very hard to conceal how mad she was.

"I called you."

"Yeah?"

"We're going to be late. I'm supposed to be there at seven."

"It's only seven-fifteen. I'll have you there by seven-thirty."

"I have to drive the SUV. I'm the president; I need to be there on time, plus I'm bringing folding chairs."

That was disappointing; he'd hoped they'd roar up in the Triumph, make an entrance, and impress all those sorors.

Trisha returned inside, leaving Jordan to himself. He

again admired the ocean view. At night it was even more beautiful, with the city lights running to the ocean and farther, all the way to the Christmas-tree bulbs of the oil derricks.

He heard a door slam and turned, expecting to see Trisha, but a man walked out of the glare of the floodlights ringing the driveway. He came over and thrust his hand at Jordan with authority, like he was used to establishing pecking order. He was tall and trim and seemed very serious for a man in baggy plaid shorts and a striped golf shirt.

"Al Bell," he said, as they shook hands.

"Jordan Davis, pleased to meet you, sir."

"Trisha tells me you teach at the university."

"Only part time. I'm a visiting lecturer."

"Good, good . . . need more young black men at the university."

He nodded and left Jordan there as he walked down the driveway to retrieve the newspaper; he nodded again as he returned to the house. Jordan got the feeling that those nods were hard for Al Bell and that it took a real effort for him to be social. What did Trisha mention he did, some kind of engineer? A moment later the garage door slowly lurched open and Trisha waved as she backed out the SUV.

They arrived at the university almost as quickly as he would have done red-lining the Triumph. Trisha seemed to know shortcuts only locals would know, and she was unafraid to floor the SUV. She was silent as she roared along, attempting to make up the time Jordan had lost for her. The dance was to be held at the Café International, where most of the minority organizations on campus had their events. Café International was large enough to house the small number of black folk on campus. She pulled up to the rear of the building, and before Jordan could unfasten the seat belt, Trisha had already bolted, running in heels across the loose gravel of the parking lot to the doors. He thought of following her but then decided to bring some of the folding chairs stacked in the rear of the SUV. He managed to fit three chairs under each arm. At the café two young women in sleek black dresses huddled behind Trisha as she knelt in front of a door, struggling with a key.

"Hi," he said, as he rested the chairs against the wall.

"Hello," the two women replied in dry, distracted unison.

"Can't get the door open?" Jordan said, confidently stating the obvious.

"Stupid office gave me the wrong key," Trisha said.

He squatted next to her and gave the key a try. It didn't fit. "Call the campus police. They have the master key," he said, remembering how he had managed to lock himself out of his office one late evening.

"Good idea," Trisha said, and she and her flock of sorors headed off to get a cell phone from a car. Jordan felt satisfied, having come up with a solution to a potentially dance-wrecking problem. Trisha and her girlfriends had to be impressed. He stood there feeling good about himself, and then he noticed a tall, well-built man walking to the café. He looked very dapper, sporting a fedora, a jacket nonchalantly slung over his shoulder like a model from a Banana Republic poster.

"Trisha around?" he asked.

"Yeah, she's making a call to get the door open," Jordan answered.

"Oh," he said, drily.

After a minute or two, Jordan wondered if this asshole realized he was being impolite, ignoring him as though he wasn't worth a stray word or two.

"Jordan," Jordan said, thrusting his hand at him as Trisha's father had done to him earlier.

"David," David said, looking bemused that Jordan wanted to shake his hand. Jordan did, doing his best to wring David's fingers a bit.

"You're helping set up?"

"Not if I can help it."

Not if he could help it? He must have watched a lot of *Masterpiece Theater* with that phony-assed English accent. Seems like everybody's got an accent these days, Jordan thought.

A campus patrol car rolled up along the access road and stopped a few yards from the café. Jordan stepped out of the shadows into the lighted walkway and gestured to the approaching campus cop.

"Here," he said, pointing to the Café International.

The cop paused, then David followed Jordan into the light. There they were, two tall black men and a lone white campus cop, assessing the situation.

"There's a dance tonight. For the Alpha Kappa Alpha Sorority," Jordan said, as pleasantly as he could manage, but the campus policeman still looked tense. Maybe he was expecting to see young women, overdressed blond sorority sisters readying for a beer bust or something.

"You two aren't in that sorority?" the cop said, jokingly, but it didn't come across as very amusing.

"No," David said, "I've never had the pleasure of pledging a sorority. Is that something you've done?"

27

Chilly. David's accent and sarcasm weren't totally lost on the campus cop. The cop didn't say anything. Jordan was sure the campus cop was thinking of how much trouble it would be to roust them. Jordan started to backpedal; he didn't need this, and he certainly didn't need this because of a snotty Anglophile with a phony-ass accent.

"Thank God," a voice exclaimed from behind them. It was Trisha and her two girlfriends. Almost instantly the mood changed. The cop relaxed and approached them without any of the hesitation he had with Jordan and David.

"Over here," Trisha said, pointing to the door. The cop walked by them without a stray glance. He was focused totally on the women, even trying to make small talk.

"Can't have a dance if you can't open the door," he said, laughing to himself and making a big production of preparing to kneel, and having to adjust the police belt with the accoutrements of his trade. By penlight, he flipped through a fat ring of keys until he found the right one and opened the door with a sweeping gesture.

"Thank you," Trisha said, so relieved to have the door open she gave the campus cop a hug.

"Good night," he said, gallantly tipping an imaginary hat to the ladies.

"I can't stand it when they get friendly," David said, more to himself than to Jordan.

The lights flashed on inside and the women started to work while David and Jordan stood outside ignoring each other. After a few minutes had gone by, Jordan could hear the sound of tables being dragged to new positions and chairs being arranged. He knew they needed help with the work, but he wanted to see if David would lift a hand, if he didn't shame him first. Then Trisha came outside.

"Are you two going to help?"

"Sure," Jordan said, embarrassed, and trudged into the café.

Trisha and David lingered by the door. He didn't see why it should, but it bothered him that she seemed so excited to see David. He forced himself out of range of their conversation, and shooed aside one of Trisha's sorors in a snug backless dress, struggling to drag a table. Unassisted, he carried it to the other side of the room. The soror followed, gesturing to help, but he refused. She was very attractive, the kind of girl who would have ignored him in high school. She wore her hair back in an intricate braid. She was almond-eyed and full-lipped, small-breasted and high-assed.

"I'm Jordan Davis," he said, extending his hand.

"Michelle," she said, barely touching it. "Trisha talks about you a lot," she drawled.

Refusing to even flirt? Trisha sure had the sorors in line, he thought. The other soror was just as pretty, but carried herself with a gruff manner and seemed obsessed with spacing chairs just so.

The room was just about ready. The center was cleared of tables and chairs, and enough seats were lined up for the wall-flowers.

"From Pic 'N' Save?" he heard Trisha say.

"Yeah, Debbie said the chips were cheaper," Michelle said with that drawl.

"I guess there's nothing wrong with trying to save a dollar," Trisha replied.

Jordan laughed to himself; Trisha never had to.

"Would you stay here with Jordan?" Jordan heard Trisha ask David.

"Stay?" Jordan said, and stepped outside to join the conversation.

"Yeah," Trisha said, taking his hand. "Michelle wants to do something with my hair. She thinks I need help."

"It's not all that," Michelle said.

"We'll be gone about an hour. You'll wait for the refreshments?" Trisha asked.

David rolled his eyes.

30

"I think I'll go with you, I have to make a run to the lab," he said, disdainfully, as though hanging with Jordon would be like viewing an unflushed toilet.

"You'll stay and let people know we'll be right back?" Trisha asked Jordan.

"I don't have much of a choice. My car's at your house."

Trisha laughed, and they left, and David went with them, managing to slyly slip an arm around Trisha's shoulders.

"Asshole," Jordan thought.

After fifteen minutes of feeling bad for himself, Jordan made a dash to the coffee nosh across the plaza. He got a large French roast and hurried back, hoping that they'd be back or that there would be pretty girls setting up bowls of cheese puffs and punch. The room was empty. He sat sipping coffee and reading a day-old paper. This David guy had to go. Sure, Jordan knew he didn't have a claim on Trisha. He wasn't even sure he wanted that, but he damn sure didn't want to have David stepping into the scene.

Finally they returned: Michelle came in first, then the gruff soror; Trisha followed with David escorting her. She had been transformed; off with the pink and green! She, too, wore a slinky, curve-hugging dress almost identical to Michelle's, and her hair was pulled back in a similar fashion. They could have been sisters if not twins. Trisha exulted in her new image.

"You look great," Jordan said.

"Thanks," she replied, and he wanted to add another compliment, but David guided her away.

Outside, Jordan felt relieved. It was ridiculous. How could he get unnerved so quickly? He walked across campus to the south-facing bluffs and looked at the silvery ocean and the moonlight casting on the breaking waves, just like he did a couple of years or so ago, when the Jamaican woman dumped him and he lost his appetite for weeks and couldn't sleep. For the first time in his life he understood what it was to be truly depressed; lying in the dark, despondently listening to Al Green and Sade. He wanted more than anything to avoid that again; he was just about sick of those CDs. He spent a miserable twenty minutes thinking of how to bum a ride home, and wondering how he could have fallen for Trisha. Was it just jealousy? He didn't want this, to live life like a zombie, unable to enjoy anything, not a newspaper, not a latte, not good Thai food, used bookstores, hikes above the hills of Santa Barbara, or running along the beach.

He didn't want to be in love.

He returned to a bustling Café International, where more than a dozen well-dressed black women were busy hanging streamers and balloons, and their men were helping in the work. Even David busied himself setting up the sound system.

31

"Where'd you go?"

It was Trisha. She looked a little worried.

"I just went for a walk," he said, shrugging.

"I wanted to introduce you to some more of my friends."

"How about a little later. Want some punch?"

"Sure," she said.

He walked to the refreshment table feeling better about himself. He could compete with David.

Trisha accepted the drink and thanked him warmly, but she only sipped at the punch.

"You don't like the punch?" Jordan asked.

"Oh, somebody poured liquor into it. Rum, I think. I'm waiting on the sodas that are supposed to be coming."

He could hardly taste the liquor.

"I'll be with you soon. We're almost finished with getting the room ready," she said, squeezing his hand.

She smiled and returned to her sorors.

He found a seat in an out-of-the-way location and hoped that the lights would dim, and the party would start to get him over this wave of jealousy.

After his fifth glass of rum punch he began to feel a little comfortable. Trisha finished with the duties of sorority president and sat next to him, resting her head on his shoulder. The music made it impossible for conversation, even though they sat far from the speakers. That was okay. He didn't want to talk. He realized something, and it felt good to revel in it; he was in the presence of more black people than he could remember, a black island in an ocean of white people that was life in Santa Barbara. Trisha, this woman of clean living, upper-middle-class bearing, was the passport from his comfortable

32

but barren isolation. She had discovered black community in the whitest of places.

"Thanks for inviting me," he whispered to Trisha.

She smiled, gripped his hand, and led him to the dance floor for one of the few slow-dance songs.

"Be patient, young man," she sang to him, and put her head on his shoulder. They moved in clumsy circles, kissing discreetly.

CHAPTER 3

Trisha wondered how she could have made such a stupid mistake. What was she trying to do to herself, inviting both Jordan and David to the same Martin Luther King Day march? David had been calling, and she didn't want to appear to be totally avoiding him. He wanted to spend time with her in the worst way, which was about as different as it could get from how things used to be. Before, it was she who was the one working overtime to be with him.

She was lost, good and lost, way out beyond Ellwood Beach, driving in the inky blackness of the boonies. Straining as hard she could to find the right address, she wanted to turn around and drive to the King Day march and forget about him. David rented a room on what had to be the darkest road in Goleta—and it wasn't really a road, just dirt, potholes, and gravel. She was just about ready to give up and head back to a gas station phone when light flooded in, blinding her.

"Hey, girl . . ."

It was David trying to catch his breath. "I've been running like ass off trying to catch you," he shouted through the rolled-up window.

He turned off the big Maglite he held in his hand like it was Darth Maul's lightsaber, and waited for Trisha to let him into the car. She barely had caught her breath from being so startled; finally calm, she opened the door and shouted at him.

"I couldn't see a thing. I was going crazy," she said.

"Oh, that's what I like around here. It's so private. No one spies on you, because they can't see," David said, like a man of mystery.

Finally, the freeway entrance and the light of civilization shining in the distance. Even though she had her attention on driving, she could feel David's eyes riveted on her.

"So, what's with this Jordan guy? Isn't he a little old for you?"

"Old? He's only twenty-eight."

"Really? Who would have guessed it. Maybe he drinks."

Trisha decided not to respond.

"So, who else is going to be at the march?"

"Michelle said she'd come and some of the other sorors."

"Michelle? I don't know about her. She's pretty and all but she's too forward."

"Too forward? Michelle?"

"She expects too much. I don't mind going out with her and all but she wants what she can't have."

"David, you guys haven't gone out but a couple of times. How do you know all this?"

"I know. We've talked. She let me know right off how much she wanted a family."

"When we first went out, all you talked about was wanting a family. Bet you did the same with Michelle."

"You think you know me so well," he said, grinning. "But between you and me it's different. We understand the same things. We come from a similar background."

Trisha could hardly wait for the Garden exit. Whenever David started in on how they were cut from the same cloth, she felt like screaming. They crossed Milpas and could see the marchers gathering in front of the Afro-American Community Center.

"Is this Jordan coming?" David asked.

"I don't know. I've invited lots of people."

"So, you invited the both of us?"

Trisha sighed. David just didn't know when to quit.

"We'll park here," Trisha said and, as quickly as she could, cut the engine, grabbed for her purse, and slammed the car door shut. She started walking, hoping David wouldn't continue to piss her off. He caught up with her and wrapped an arm around her shoulders and kissed her on the cheek. David had such a selective memory. What was she supposed to think about this new and improved attitude? Before he went away to England, about the only time he called was to borrow money. *Oh, it's only for the short term. Dad said he'd send the money.* But Dad didn't, and she had loaned David more than a thousand dollars of her own money over the last two years. He had yet to repay her a cent. It was like she was helping to finance his undergraduate education.

"People like us understand what the score is. Our parents accomplished much and we have to do just as much."

Trisha shrugged as they entered the crowd of marchers and she slipped away from his grasp. She made her way to the very end of the hundred or so people, almost all of Santa Barbara's black community, plus the last few remaining white members of the local NAACP. Most everyone was a family friend or an acquaintance of some sort. Her hunch paid off; at the rear of the marchers she found Jordan lingering dead last. He was obviously daydreaming, oblivious to the lighting of the candles to commence the march.

"Jordan!"

Trisha reached over and squeezed his hand.

"Have you seen my mother?"

"Yeah, I did. Walking with a huge candle she had to hold with two hands. She had to ask someone to hold it so she could give me a hug."

"She really likes you."

Jordan shrugged nervously.

"You want to get something to eat after this?" he asked.

"Maybe later. I've got to give a friend a ride home," she said.

Just then the procession started to move. All the candle holders gathered at the head of the march and led the way for the rest of them.

"See, in L.A. we didn't celebrate King Day. We would just caravan to the beach and get toasted."

"Oh, don't be such a cynic. Come on, help me find my mother."

Jordan allowed Trisha to pull him into the heart of the march. Then, almost at the front of the slowly moving crowd, she suddenly stopped, causing folks behind them to stumble. Jordan saw what caused her to lose her balance; David was with Lady Bell, the both of them looking regal and self-assured as he escorted her and her huge candle to the very front of the line.

"That's your stuck-up friend, David. That boy's everywhere."

"Well, he came with me."

"What? I thought you asked me."

"Yeah, I did, but you never did confirm."

Jordan shook his head. "Confirm?"

"In my world people do confirm," Trisha said.

"How far is the march?"

"To State Street, but we couldn't get a permit to march down State Street, said it would be too disruptive."

"Those bastards!"

"Are you ever serious?"

"As a heart attack."

They continued on into the dense core of marchers. There, she waved to a heavyset black woman done up like she was ready for church, in a fur and a kind of beehive wig.

"Pie!" Trisha shouted.

"Y'all late!" Pie said, frowning.

"I know. The parking was horrible," Trisha answered.

"Y'all still late."

Trisha gave Pie a kiss and wrapped her arms around Pie's wide waist. Pie smiled happily and handed each of them a candle. "Y'all should know what to do with these."

Jordan thought Pie's voice was better for croaking than

39

talking. Listening to her made him want to laugh, but he had sense enough not to do something that stupid.

"Pie, this is Jordan. He teaches at the university."

"Pleased to meet you, Mrs. Pie," Jordan said, nervously.

"You sure about that?" Pie drawled.

He extended his hand to her, and she examined it for a moment and dropped it.

"How you know I've been married?"

"Huh?"

"You called me Mrs. How you don't know I just don't shack up or what?"

"I just assumed . . ."

She laughed. "You sound like a smart boy. Is he smart?"

Trisha didn't seem flustered a bit by Pie asking such a question. Jordan was, though.

"What, y'all expecting to get engaged but you ain't brought him 'round to see me."

"Excuse me, ma'am," Jordan said, glancing at Trisha.

"I like this boy. He's got manners. But you better tell him why you can't cook."

"Pie helped raise us. She did all the cooking."

"Raise y'all? I been working for the Bell family since 1975. I was the first one to take you home. You was the prettiest and the cryin'ist baby I ever want to see. That family is the quietest colored folk I ever done worked for. I cooked, cleaned those Bell babies' butts, but Trisha done take the cake. You got both these boys trying to make time with you. You got nerve."

Luckily for Trisha and Jordan the march started, and Pie saw friends further along and left them without a backward glance.

Soon they arrived at State Street and the short march ended in front of the popular Joe's Bar and Grill, where Lady Bell held her candle up high, and David stood next to a tall minister with a booming voice who led them in prayer for the memory of Dr. King.

Afterward, Jordan took Trisha's hand.

"Let's go to that Thai place you like."

Before she could respond, David appeared, standing a bit out of earshot, wearing a bemused expression. The march ended quickly but not quickly enough. Trisha wanted to drop David off in Goleta and return to Jordan as quickly as she could, but first she had to maneuver around the minefield of good-byes, especially with Pie returning their way.

"I'm inviting you young people to my place for Sock It to Me Cake."

Trisha shook her head. "I've got to get David home. He's studying for medical school exams."

"He can study after he eat," Pie said. Trisha knew that it was impossible to argue with her once she got going. Then David added his two cents.

"Sock It to Me Cake sounds good. I'm taking a break."

Trisha shrugged. David was never that generous or easy when she had been crazy about him.

"Okay, I've got to get back and grade some papers," Jordan said, and took off so fast she wondered if he heard her good-bye.

As Trisha drove to Pie's, she refused to say a word. David, though, chattered relentlessly.

"I don't know what you see in this Jordan. He really is stuck on himself."

"Jordan? I always thought you loved yourself more than you ever loved me."

David sighed, dramatically.

There was a pause. She didn't want drama with him; all she wanted was to drop him off and get the hell back on the freeway without getting lost on those dark roads.

"You really like this guy?"

It was like he hadn't heard a word she said.

"I like him a lot," she said, and instantly regretted it.

David sighed again, dramatically.

"It's so obvious. But it can't work out. You should be able to see that."

Trisha refused to take the bait and turned off the road into Pie's driveway. She lived on the lower east end of Santa Barbara, an area older locals referred to as Little Mexico. Ironically, Pie's property extended all the way to Coast Village Road, the main drag of Montecito, which meant this old black woman who could barely read was property rich. Trisha liked the Mexican neighborhood with all those friendly kids, some as brown as she was, playing in flower-filled yards. She wished she was back there and not having to escort David into Pie's cramped living room. They sat on the annoyingly soft vinyl-covered couch, and already the backs of her thighs were sweating. She couldn't keep upright enough to avoid leaning on David, which inspired him to slip his arm around her. Tommy, Pie's old gutbucket ex-Marine, had his attention focused on the prizefight happening on his stomach; his preferred way to watch his five-inch television was to rest it on his stomach, and if people came by, he'd put it at an angle so they could see a bit. The real action wasn't on that silly television but in the kitchen; Pie and Lady Bell were banging pots and swinging pans. Trisha wanted to leave but she was stuck until the desserts were ready. Also, she couldn't figure out why David, the world's most bitterly impatient person, sat happily sorting through a stack of *Jet* magazines, sipping a big tumbler of Kool-Aid that Pie had poured for him.

"Mom! You have to explain to Pie why I have to go."

Lady Bell appeared in the doorway, drying her flour-encrusted hands on the worn apron.

"Well, . . . Pie. These kids need to be on their way."

"Aw, I want y'all to have some cake. It's just about ready. Hold your horses and there's a cake for your daddy too," Pie said, and returned to the kitchen.

43

Trisha knew what that meant. Daddy must be in another bad mood and she was elected to lead the food appeasement detail. She'd probably be the one who'd have to bring it into the den where he'd be glaring at the television. Why did he need his own cake? So he could eat and glower without having to share? She caught David smiling at her.

"What are you grinning at?" she snarled.

"Can't you relax? That cake smells delicious. I'm content to wait."

"I am waiting," she said angrily.

After another fifteen minutes Pie came out with a tray of fat slices of very yellow cake, and as soon as Pie returned to the kitchen, Trisha glared at David.

"Eat the cake!" she said.

She ate two tart bites and headed for the door.

"Come on, David!" she demanded, waving at him.

Trisha had started the engine and put it into reverse before looking up at David peering anxiously into the window. She finally unlocked the door, let him in, and drove recklessly to the freeway, speeding all the way out to Goleta in silence.

"I can't believe you're acting so love struck!" David said.

"Who's acting love struck?"

"Don't lie, but he's not your kind."

"You keep talking about kind. Are you supposed to be my kind? Am I supposed to be happy about that?"

"Yes, you should, because we have a chance for a future. That's what's important."

"I don't know how you could say that. David, we broke it off before you went to England. Nothing's changed."

"Yes, it has. I've changed."

"How?"

"I want to marry you."

"You'd better get out here," she said, and stopped abruptly. She unlocked the door without pulling over to the side of the road.

"Trisha?"

She looked straight ahead, ignoring David. Finally he sighed and put one foot out of the car. Trisha smashed the gas pedal, and David had to leap away, fearing for his leg, if not his life.

Trisha drove home on automatic pilot, so overwhelmed with David's marriage proposal that she didn't notice the trash cans in front of the garage door until she hit them, but not so hard as to do damage to either the car or the door but more than loud enough to irritate her father. After she cut the engine and the lights, she slumped in the seat and waited for him to come peering out. She dreaded having to contend with his bad temper. Sure enough the door opened, and she watched him silhouetted in the doorway, hands on hips. How long did he plan on staying there like some damn motionless sentinel?

"Trisha, is that you? Why the hell are you driving like a lunatic?"

Suddenly, she wasn't afraid of his temper; she didn't care. She was an adult and he needed to respect that, even if she did run over the trash cans. She walked by him with a curt "Good night" and headed for her bedroom. She had no time to worry about her father, when she had David to worry about.

"Because you're a Christian. You believe in family, and you know what we're working toward because we both come from there to start with," David had said to her on more than one occasion. That was his justification for the relationship, even when he insisted they were still a couple, after she had wanted to end it earlier on.

Then almost instantly she was angry. How could he treat her like shit for so long and then expect her to marry him? And she wanted to ask, "So what about all these rumors about how wild you were in England? You're the one who says he's such a Christian!"

She hoped that by lying perfectly still in bed she might fall asleep, but she became even more alert. She detested the fact that David still had such influence over her, but perversely she couldn't help imagining herself and David five years from now; she'd be finished with law school and David with his internship at some prestigious hospital, and then they'd squeeze in two beautiful kids and live like the Kennedys or something.

45

They shared a mutual fantasy of achievement and wealth that each made more possible for the other. Her own fantasies made her queasy; thinking about his made her depressed.

She immediately called Jordan.

"Jordan?"

"Trisha? What's up?"

"Oh, nothing much. I just needed to hear your voice."

"Really, that's nice to know."

"Are you busy?"

"Oh no, I was thinking of slipping out . . . for a beer. It's not really late."

"I'd like to see you."

"Yeah." Jordan paused long enough to sink Trisha's heart. "Sure, I can swing by. You want to go to Frimples for a burger?"

"I shouldn't leave. My father is a little paranoid about me being out late. I thought we could talk for a minute. I'll meet you in the driveway. Don't ring the bell. I'll hear you."

Trisha hung up, relieved to know she'd see him; she didn't need a scene with her father, but one was coming. She had to get her own apartment. She couldn't manage her life and him too. He needed so much order in his life the whole family tried as best they could to conceal whatever might upset him. Footsteps stopped at her door. "Good night, sugar," Lady Bell said. Mother knew how to do it, slip into the house without making a sound, and since she slept in a separate bedroom, she could avoid causing those little disturbances Daddy couldn't tolerate. It used to be easier when she was a girl. During all those business trips for General Electric he took, her mother had the opportunity to run the house as she saw fit, and backed with the checkbook, almost anything went if it had to do with church, or civil rights, or the down-and-out. Trisha remembered when she let the Black Student Union have their meeting at the house, but Pie had to tell her that those funny cigarettes were marijuana.

"Lady Bell, we got to get them to clear out of here! They smoking funny cigarettes!" While her mother was horrified, waving her hands over her head like she was shooing flies, Pie managed to herd two dozen buzzed college students from the living room without offending anyone. If Lady Bell had a special power, it was being incapable of giving or receiving offense . . . and charming everyone.

Even through the heavy curtains Trisha heard the distant, faint roar of the bad muffler of Jordan's Triumph. She hurried through the house to disarm the security alarm and then went outside, hoping to meet him at the bottom of the driveway. Before she was halfway down she saw headlights flying up the hill, but then to her relief he cut his lights and engine and coasted to a stop a few yards from the house. She ran to the car gesturing for him to follow.

"Let's go sit by the pool," she whispered.

Jordan shrugged and followed her along the side of the house to the pool deck. She led him to the lawn chairs farthest from the house.

"Great view," he said, whispering as he looked down at the flickering lights of the city and the happy Christmas lights of the drilling platforms in the channel.

"We can talk here. It's far enough from the house."

"Oh, that's good. It's beautiful tonight, full moon. I bet you have a lot of coyotes up here."

"I've never noticed."

"Coyotes are the pimps of the ecosystem. Eating people's cats and those little dogs I can't stand."

Jordan paused and looked around at Trisha's house.

"By the way, what does your father do to make the money for all this?"

"Oh, he's an executive for General Electric."

"Yeah?"

"He's into power systems sales."

"Oh, that sounds impressive."

Trisha scooted her chair a little closer to his.

"What do you think of David?"

He laughed.

"David? What am I supposed to think of him? Am I supposed to think something about him?"

"What kind of man do you think he is?"

"I don't know. He seems okay if you like that kind of person."

"What do you mean?"

"He's handsome and well-spoken, but you know he's a little stuck on himself."

"There's some truth in that."

"The question is, why are you asking me?"

"He asked me a question tonight and I just wanted to know your opinion."

"He asked you to marry him?"

"Yes, he did."

"You're joking, right?"

"No."

Jordan smiled and sat back in his chair.

"So, what did you say?"

"I didn't say a thing."

"Really? You want to be married to him?"

"I don't know. I have to think about it."

Jordan slipped his arm around her.

"You don't want to marry him."

"How do you know?"

"Well, for one thing, you like me."

"So? Maybe I want to be married."

"You're too young. What, twenty-three years old and ready to settle down?"

"I believe in long engagements."

"So do I."

"Do you ever think about marriage?" Trisha asked.

"Only in the abstract."

"Maybe David is my only option."

"You'll have plenty of other options. Plus, it's pretty obvious about David."

"What's obvious?"

"He's gay."

"Gay? You don't know David. He's not gay. That's out of the question."

"Maybe you don't know the right questions," Jordan said.

"I was serious with David for almost two years."

"I'm not trying to say something bad about David. Soon as he said a word I assumed he was gay."

"What does that say about me? That because I'm not experienced I can't tell if a man is gay?"

"I don't think it says anything. If David turns out to be straight I'm not going to shoot myself, but you know, some men do that. They want the best of both worlds on the down low."

Jordan stood and led Trisha to the edge of the deck, which provided the best view of the ocean. He kissed her.

"You should come spend the night at my house," Jordan said.

"I'd like to but I can't."

"Where there's a will, there's a way . . . you know."

"Do you always talk this way? You're never serious."

"You just aren't paying attention. I'm always serious."

Jordan pulled away from Trisha as though his feelings were hurt. She ignored him and rested her head against his chest.

"So, you have any idea when you'll be ready to settle down?"

"You know . . . out of all the women I've dated, you're the only one who's so up front about marriage. It's sort of refreshing."

"You're pushing thirty."

"Hey, I'm twenty-eight. Thirty is two years from now. I'm still good to go."

"Things do happen."

"Soon as I've decided to tie the knot I'll give you a call."

"Give you a call? Why would I want to hear from you if you're getting married."

"Maybe I'll be calling for another reason. Maybe I'll be calling for you," he said, with an arched eyebrow, and tried to kiss her again. She pulled away, gasping.

"I'm okay. . . . I forgot to breathe."

Jordan laughed.

"You're like a character out of a Victorian novel. You sure your corset isn't on too tight?"

Trisha pushed him away.

"You make me nervous."

"Me? I'm harmless."

A light in the den of the house came on and Trisha froze.

"My father's awake."

"Is that a cause for alarm? Does he have a gun?"

"Stop joking."

"Who's joking?"

"You should go. Can you drive quietly?"

"Wow, you demand a lot of a brother with a messed-up muffler."

He gave her a quick kiss and walked quickly to the Triumph.

He took off the brake and coasted downhill, hardly making a sound.

Trisha saw her father in his pajamas and robe, peering through the open sliding-glass doors with a golf club in his hand, looking a little silly, but dignified in his silliness.

"Hi, Dad," she said. "I couldn't sleep so I'm getting some air."

"Were you out front?"

"Me, no."

"I thought I heard something out front."

"Maybe coyotes?"

He shrugged.

"Do they come around here?"

"They're all over the place."

He eyed his golf club as if he needed something more substantial.

"Good night," she said, and went to bed.

CHAPTER 4

Jordan's worst fear was that he'd have too few students and the Japanese literature class that he had wanted to teach for the last two years would be canceled; then he'd have to scrounge up a composition class or he'd be back at the Hour Glass scrubbing hot tubs. He was right; not one student filled a seat in the dimly lit room. This was serious and something drastic had to be done; or he'd be showing horny couples to their steaming, overchlorinated hot tubs, and afterward cleaning up their empty beer bottles and used condoms. Even Provost Mudrick couldn't keep an empty class open. After rearranging his notes on the *Tale of Genji* and *The Makioka Sisters,* he reexamined the enrollment papers; seven people had signed up. Where were they? Disgusted, he headed for the halls to see if he could talk some soft-hearted student into adding his class, but the hallway was just about as deserted as the classroom.

Then his attention was seized by a tall, shapely woman with her hair pulled back in a loose braid that hung to her shoulders. Dressed in narrow, pleated gabardine pants, a striped blouse, and pumps, she stood out as a beacon of fashion among the post-hippies and sorority chicks. Her attention was focused on the class descriptions posted on the far wall. He watched her, wanting to see her face clearly, wondering if it was as attractive as her figure.

"Need some help?" Jordan finally asked.

She turned to answer, but his question was answered before she said a word. She was beautiful.

He tried to place her. Maybe she was foreign, maybe Ethiopian and white, something . . . Her coloring, even in the bad fluorescent lighting, was like rich honey. He wondered if it was natural, or did she fry herself sitting long hours in the sun to achieve one of Santa Barbara's most important assets, a perfect tan. Her hair was kind of unruly, with curls dangling in her face. She shook her head and he saw that the hair concealed very pretty gray-green eyes.

She smiled generously.

"I'm looking for a Japanese lit class."

"I'm the—you know—teaching that class."

"Great."

He led the way to the class trying to look professional and not almost giddy to have a student, and a beautiful student at that.

Seated, he flipped through the fat volume of *Tale of Genji,* keeping his eyes on the pages as they flipped back and forth.

He didn't want to look at her and maybe make her uncomfortable.

"Are you a history major?" he asked.

"No, literature."

"You look foreign."

"I do?"

He realized he was babbling badly and making a fool of himself. He looked away from her and fumbled nervously with his notes about the Seidensticker translation of *Tale of Genji*.

"How did you get interested in Japanese literature?" she asked, pleasantly, as though rambling like an idiot wasn't a bad thing. He tried to pull himself from the quicksand of his stupidity.

"Watching samurai films, going to sushi bars, gambling, and tattoos—the low-brow approach to culture," he said, again worried that he was rambling.

"What about you?" he asked, grasping again for land.

"I love reading, and Japanese literature appeals to me."

He felt himself looking at her like some pathetic puppy.

Two students walked in. At first he was relieved, knowing he had already blown it with her. He hurriedly welcomed them, gave each a syllabus, and pointed to the registration information on the board, but his attention returned like a homing pigeon to the woman.

"I didn't get your name," he asked tentatively, as though he had no right to ask.

"Daphne Daniels."

He reached to shake her hand, but in the three years of teaching at the university, it had never occurred to him to shake any student's hand. Daphne smiled at him as if she understood his discomfort. Finally, he pulled himself together enough to start the class, but it was an unbearable tightrope walk. He wouldn't even look in Daphne's direction for fear he'd be paralyzed once again. All he could manage was to go over the course syllabus, word for word, as though they weren't capable of reading it for themselves. Usually, he would start with a phrase or two in Japanese, but somehow his Japanese fled and then his English abandoned him too. After forty minutes, it occurred to him to end the class. The students asked their last few questions about the *Tale of Genji* and the other assigned texts, but Jordan didn't hear them; his attention had flown with Daphne, who had magically slipped out.

CHAPTER 5

She was hopelessly late; somehow she couldn't get out the
door. No matter how she tried, she couldn't get it
together; stockings shredded if she put a foot in them, her
hair had frizzled up until it looked like a sad Afro, and she
fucked up making coffee, spilling it all over the kitchen
floor. Maybe if she hadn't stayed up until 3:30 reading
the last three hundred pages of *Genji*, she wouldn't feel
like shit.

One more cigarette before heading out. The sun shining
through the glass of the enclosed porch was so intoxicating she
couldn't rush. She thought of him again, and the fact that
halfway through the quarter he had yet to make a pass, even
though his crush was very obvious. Last week he tried to explain something about Japanese court life and glanced at her

and started stuttering. The other students had to think that they were seeing each other.

She thought they would be going out too, but he was shy, and she was hesitant. She hadn't dated a black man before. She was who she was, uncomfortable on both sides; once white men realized that she was a quarter African, they changed toward her, like she was withholding some aspect of her personality, that at any moment she might spontaneously start doing an African fertility dance. She assumed that most men thought of her as exotic, as if they wanted to claim her for their tribe. Jordan didn't seem like that; she genuinely liked him. Maybe it was because he seemed to have fallen for her so quickly and hard, but didn't inflict it on her. He kept it to himself.

She wanted to keep her life as calm as possible and to do that meant keeping her parents calm. Nothing agitated them more than her choice in men, especially after Frank, but Jordan they would have to approve of, if it got to that.

Time had gotten away from her again. Twenty minutes to the hour and she had yet to leave the house. She rushed for the door but her mother burst in before she could reach it.

"Daphne! I'll need help tonight."

"I'll be there," she said, slipping by her mother, clutching books, purse, and coffee mug to her chest, juggling them all the way to her Volvo. She searched through her purse for keys and for a minute thought they were in another purse, but she found them wrapped in a wad of tissue.

Wet! At least an inch of water pooled up from the floorboards as a result of last night's unexpected rain and the open sunroof. Her shoes were soaked, but she had no time to do anything but drive if she wanted to get to class before it was over.

Everywhere she looked on campus, cars were jockeying for parking spots. So hopeless a situation she gave up and resigned herself to the long walk with sopping, squeaking heels. She found a spot by the lagoon that had a view of the bluffs' choppy, rain-swollen ocean. She had to remember to close the sunroof if it looked like rain. Did it look like rain now? She left the sunroof open.

The walk to class took less time than she remembered, but still she was later than her worse projections, and she still couldn't go to class without stopping in the rest room to see if she could do something about making herself more presentable. She darted from the rest room and headed for the class. No matter how much she wanted to go home she couldn't give in to the impulse; everything falls apart so quickly. At the end of the short hallway to the class she couldn't bring herself to make a left. Stuck ridiculously on the verge of turning the corner, she couldn't bring herself to move. Approaching footsteps propelled her on. She saw Jordan in front of the class, books in hand, resting against the door. Maybe she could slip away.

"Hey, Daphne, I've been waiting on you."

"Me?" Her heart sank. What had she done? "Waiting on me?"

"Remember? Class is in the library so we can look at the reproductions of the Genji Scrolls."

"Really?"

"I . . . you know . . . didn't want you to miss it. The scrolls are beautiful, and I had a feeling you had forgotten that we're supposed to meet there."

Daphne waited for him to lead the way but instead he looked at her feet.

"Your shoes are squeaking."

"No they're not," she mumbled.

"Oh," Jordan replied as they headed for the library.

She walked beside him trying not to draw more attention to her feet.

It was a short walk to the art library, but they still arrived at the special collections room almost forty minutes late. No one from the class was there at the meeting place but Daphne could see that Jordan was delighted to have her to himself.

"This wasn't a mandatory meeting. I hope some people went ahead and checked out the scrolls without me."

The special collections librarian found the heavy, over-sized book and led them to a windowless room.

"You have a half hour before the next class. I'll knock when your time is up."

As soon as the door was closed, Jordan grinned. He flipped open the book and pointed to various prints of Genji chasing kimono-clad geishas. While they examined the prints, Daphne felt Jordan's arm pressing against hers. She wondered how long he would keep it there. She didn't mind the contact; it endeared him more to her. He came on like a high school kid. It seemed ironic that he was so fascinated with this randy Genji, and yet he couldn't bring himself to take the next step in dating a student. The way it's done, he must ask her out for coffee to discuss something incomprehensible: (I'd like to get your opinion on Genji supposedly being an icon of male beauty in contrast to iconic female objectification); or something innocuous (Let's talk over your paper, just brainstorm some ideas . . .)—those were two approaches she expected. Could she bring herself to help him along? The half hour passed quickly. Would he attempt a date now before parting? The knock came for them to clear out. Jordan looked tense as though something was up. He returned the reproductions, then as they walked outside he became visibly nervous.

He cleared his throat.

She was about to ask him to call her, when he blurted it out.

"Would you like to have coffee sometime?"

"Sure," she said, with confidence.

He sighed, like life after death.

"We don't have much time to talk in class," she said.

"Tonight?" he asked.

"Great," she said, and scribbled her phone number on the back of a traffic ticket.

He looked at the ticket with surprise.

"You'll need this."

"Really?"

"Yeah, they'll impound your car."

"Somehow they get paid."

"Seven, is that good for you?"

"Fine," she said, then abruptly walked away.

Another moment of pure panic. She needed to be in the car driving south but it was debatable if she could manage to keep the panic from escalating. Last week she had to pull off the road and huddle on the floor until it passed. This time, though, as she hurried into the car, the cold surprise of the rainwater pooled onto the floorboards short-circuited the rising panic attack.

Now, feeling more reasonable, she drove home figuring ways to break her date. She had to resist that impulse to do what she knew she shouldn't, but if she begged out of seeing him, she might as well just drop the class, and she needed the class because it was another foothold up and out of the mess she had made of her life.

Instead of exiting at Mission, she drove another five miles south to the nude beach on the other side of Summerland. She needed a swim even if it was a cold, gray day. She parked above the beach, but after a short hike and a careful crossing of the rocks, she reached Boys' Beach, the gay stretch of sand where she felt more or less safe. Women who wanted to sunbathe were almost assured to be left alone if they stayed beyond the rocks. Other than a few lone strollers, the beach was nearly empty. She hid her keys beneath the towel and quickly slipped out of her dress and charged into the surf. She swam to the breakers even though the water was frigid. There, she could see the shoreline snaking back to Santa Barbara. She thought of Jordan again, which surprised her. It was a dead issue. His feelings would be hurt over the date but it was unavoidable. There was nothing she could do for him but bring him trouble.

Daphne returned home surprised to see a number of unfamiliar cars in the driveway. She didn't remember the party until it was too late to retreat to the library or café, anywhere sane. She heard laughter and looked into the living room and saw a bartender serving cocktails, but before she could slip away, her mother appeared, apron around her evening dress, and beckoned her into the kitchen.

"Daphne! Where were you? I'm shorthanded, and the Ashbys are here!"

"The Ashbys!" Daphne said, with alarm.

She looked into the room again and saw Nelly Ashby with a plate of hors d'oeuvres on her ample lap and her husband/lapdog, Bill Ashby, a diminutive, gray-haired dapper-ass. Nelly Ashby produced a soap in Los Angeles and tried to live her life in Santa Barbara as though she were a character in one. A remarkably generous woman, she contributed a great deal to the museum, but it was only a matter of time before she exploded like a horny Roman candle. Daphne wished that Nelly had something underneath her jacket because inevitably she would let it fall open to show off her prodigious breast implants.

"Make another tray of appetizers," her mother ordered, and left to work the patrons.

Well, at least she had a real excuse to give Jordan.

The night, as she expected, grew weirder: The three couples she didn't know treated her as if she were hired help. Perhaps they suspected that wonderful tan was really her natural coloration; brown like a Mexican, like a black? Even though her mother made quite an embarrassing flourish about her newfound status as a college student studying literature, just a month ago she would have introduced her as the daughter who screwed up her life. Anyway, who gave a damn about these people except for their pocketbooks, buying what little respect they had by having the good taste to throw money at culture? All their airbrushed youthfulness couldn't conceal their essential tackiness. Anyway, the fun would start soon. Each of these girlfriends or wives of these titans of industry had a boob job; it would only be a matter of time before Nelly rose to the challenge.

"Another apple martini," the dark-haired professional wife said, holding up a glass.

Daphne made sure to look straight into her eyes before committing to memory that this fish wouldn't receive another drink from her hands in this lifetime.

"Daphne! I haven't seen you since you last jumped ship. When was that, last April? I thought maybe you were sold into a white slavery ring."

Daphne shrugged; would a white slavery ring have her?

She decided not to turn to Nelly as she retrieved half-empty glasses.

"I don't know how to respond to that," she finally said.

"Oh, I'm just teasing, but it's good to have you back because, like me, you hate these frosty dot-com bitches."

Mr. Ashby looked from his gin and tonic to pat his wife's red face.

"Don't fly off the handle. No need for a scene."

"God, I'm hot in here," Nelly Ashby said, and slipped her jacket open, revealing herself to the party.

Daphne shrugged. Too predictable to be shocking, but her mother would have more than enough shock for everyone. The amusing thing was that Nelly seemed to expect a reaction, shouts of surprise, maybe indignation, but the couples continued chattering on as though the plump, sunbaked, toasted woman was invisible.

Daphne admired her breasts; they stood firm and fake as a

plaster Mount Rushmore. Through with it all, Daphne abandoned her mother downstairs to officiate the party alone.

She managed to get to class early on Thursday and found a seat near the door. Soon as he arrived, she stood to greet Jordan.

"Jordan, I'm sorry. My mother had an emergency. I had to help with a party for the art museum."

She could see the hurt in his eyes as he thought of a response.

"It's my fault and it was wrong of me not to call you. Let me make it up to you. Dinner maybe?"

He looked surprised and pleased but not entirely reassured.

"Sure, whenever. But don't feel obligated."

"Tonight?"

"Tonight?"

"Sure, if you're free. Maybe Japanese."

"That sounds fine."

Daphne turned to leave.

"What time?" he asked.

"Seven?"

"Sure."

She turned to leave again.

"Your address?"

She quickly wrote it down for him and returned to her seat. For the rest of the class she saw him looking at her, but she refused to meet his eyes, and when class ended she made a quick exit.

*   *   *

Norbert's was her favorite restaurant in Santa Barbara. The re-stored California bungalow near the beach was crowded as usual with overdressed blue-haired ladies. She needed to have a drink on the veranda surrounded by wisteria and morning glory vines, watching the sunset over the ocean. She wondered if Jordan would like to have dinner here, would he feel comfortable? Maybe he would find it silly. Her mother waited at the usual table with two glasses of wine. Daphne kissed her, then sank into the heavily cushioned rattan chair and had a long sip of wine and sighed.

"Rough day?" Mrs. Daniels asked.

Daphne shrugged and had another even longer sip of wine. "I feel dehydrated."

"How's *Genji* coming?"

"We've finished that. Now it's *The Makioka Sisters*, the *Little Women* of Japanese literature."

"Is that supposed to be a selling point?"

"It's better than that. Everyone gets diarrhea at the end."

Mrs. Daniels frowned, which surprised Daphne because her mother usually liked silliness.

"Your father received a message."

"A message?"

"Yes. It was Frank."

She slipped her hand onto Daphne's.

"We took care of it. I called back and told him I had no idea where you were. That you haven't been home since the holidays."

Daphne smiled to reassure her mother.

"He doesn't care. He has other girlfriends. He's too lazy to come the distance."

"We can get a restraining order."

"Really, it's okay. It's over."

"Yes. He probably called blind, hoping you might answer."

"I'll screen my calls for a while."

Mrs. Daniels finished her wine and asked the waiter for another glass.

"I debated not telling you. The last thing in the world I want to do is worry you. We love having you home."

"It's good being back."

Frank knew she was back. Her parents couldn't lie worth a shit, and he had powers, mind control, ESP, whatever; he had it.

"Don't worry. It'll all work out," she said, in her brightest voice for her mother's sake. That's what she learned all those years of running away; the devil may be on his way to claim your soul, but you still need new stockings and to be able to lie with a straight face.

CHAPTER 6

"A new suit? Who's this white girl that has you so sprung?" Ned asked Jordan, as Jordan admired himself in the bathroom mirror.

"She's not white. She's something. I haven't asked her."

"Man, man, man. That's interesting. You got women crawling all over you. Poor little Trisha's given up on you, and that other chick, freak-mama Mary, calls looking for you, and you don't got a minute for none of them."

"Trisha knows I'm working on my thesis."

"Yeah, you busy. Had the car washed, your hair styled, a new suit, flowers . . . please, you busy in love."

"Ned, as usual, you don't know what's happening."

"All right, then you don't mind if I ask Trisha out?"

Jordan stopped primping long enough to cut his eyes at Ned.

"That's . . . up to you. If Trisha wants to go out with you, what can I do about it? I don't have papers on her."

"Cool! Soon as you out the door I'll call her up. What's the number?"

"F-U-C-K-Y-O-U!" Jordan said.

"See, you really think you're Don Juan. All the women are yours."

"Here, I'll give you Mary's number. She's got needs bigger than all outdoors."

Jordan quickly scribbled a number and tossed it to Ned.

"You know I can't use that."

70

"Suit yourself. Just remember with her it's a sex thang."

Ned waved him off and Jordan headed for the door, but he turned and darted back in and caught Ned peering at Mary's number.

"Busted!" Jordan said.

Ned shrugged in defeat.

After driving lost on the poorly marked and badly lit roads of Hope Ranch, he found her house through dumb luck; a posting with an address for a house for sale saved him from calling for more directions. He drove up a long driveway to a Craftsman mansion, concealed almost completely by a grove of eucalyptus trees. Though he usually tried to put a price on Santa Barbara real estate, this time he just shook his head. Daphne's family was just plain rich.

Jordan parked and walked up the pebble path, annoyed at the crunching underneath his feet, as though it would draw attack dogs who'd appear snarling and frothing. He was nervous, so nervous that his stomach churned like he had had a bad burrito at lunch. To add to his nerves, he reached the porch to see a clear glass oval set in a wooden frame. He knocked and waited, hating being robbed of the few minutes he thought he would have to himself. Then he saw a woman hurrying down the stairs, but it wasn't Daphne rushing to meet him; a thin white woman smiled at him through the glass door as she unlocked it. She was attractive even in a dour dress you'd expect to see on a nun.

"Jordan? Come on in. I'm Denise Daniels, Daphne's mother," she said, extending her hand.

"Pleased to meet you," he said, smiling awkwardly.

"She's just about ready. She speaks so often of you I feel we've met."

This was new to Jordan. In his circle of university friends, everyone was from somewhere else; now it seemed all the women he felt strongly about had too much family. She led him to a couch in the jungle-theme living room, green walls and plenty of plants, even a lemon tree with lemons; horrifying Indonesian wooden busts lined the mantel above the fireplace; and a frightening freestanding fanlike sculpture, five feet high, nothing but eyes and fangs.

"Would you care for a drink?"

"Water would be nice."

Jordan watched her walk away, thinking that she seemed at ease and friendly. She returned with a goblet of sparkling water with a slice of lemon.

"Now, let me hurry Daphne. She just runs late."

She didn't have to. Daphne came down the stairs in a burgundy dress, wearing a pearl necklace, her hair cascading down in curls along her shoulders. He watched her with unbroken attention as she made her way to him.

71

"Ready?" she asked, smiling as though he was running late.

"Yeah, how about the Tokyo Inn?"

Daphne seemed surprised at the suggestion.

"That's fine with me."

"We don't have to go there."

"No, I insist."

Jordan shrugged.

A door unlocked behind him and he saw a red-faced, slump-shouldered man stumble drunkenly into the house. He ducked into the kitchen, and both mother and daughter ignored him like he was some kind of ghost.

Daphne kissed her mother good-bye, and as she and Jordan walked to the door, she smirked.

"That embarrassment is my father."

Jordan nodded, feeling awkward at being present to see the family dirty laundry; but one thing was clear, she didn't look a thing like either of her parents.

At first they rode in awkward silence. He was too nervous to make small talk but he knew he had to if the night wasn't going to die early.

"Nice home you have."

"My grandfather left it to my mother. I have a great bedroom that opens to the ocean on one side, the mountains on the other. I miss it when I travel. My grandmother was an actress, and she lost a great role because she was ill. Clark Gable came to pay a visit, and they had tea in my bedroom."

"You travel a lot?"

"I haven't been home for more than a few days in the last eight years."

"Why's that?"

"My old boyfriend is a concert promoter. We went everywhere."

The boyfriend. There had to be one lurking in the wings.

"I ran away at fifteen with my girlfriend. I had one of my parents' cars, and we pretty much lived in it until they caught up with me and took it."

Jordan nodded, waiting for Daphne to continue.

"We ran away because we wanted to do wild things. We spent more time trying to keep wild things from happening."

"I ran away to college," Jordan added.

"I was too possessed with my own idea of the world to do that."

Jordan waited for Daphne to elaborate, but she didn't.

Inside, the restaurant was near empty. This was just what he wanted, the quiet serenity of slow business. The waitress seated them next to a fifty-gallon aquarium, a convenient seat to watch the brightly colored saltwater fish.

"Dinner," he said.

She smiled, but it was so slight, he couldn't be sure.

"So about this boyfriend, you still seeing him?"

"No," she said. This time he was certain she smiled.

"Good. I thought all beautiful women came equipped with jealous boyfriends."

The waitress appeared and Daphne suggested they order the large bottle of sake, and oddball sushi he had never been inclined to eat, like uni, quail egg, and octopus, but it was only the octopus he had trouble eating. It seemed like potent, fish-flavored bubble gum that lasted longer than he could stand.

"How do you like being a student again?" he asked, deftly shooting the octopus from his mouth to the napkin.

"I like it. I was working downtown as a secretary, and that wasn't any fun."

"Why?"

"I'm not . . . the kind of person who should have jobs like that. I can't be counted on. If it's not life or death I don't care very much. Being fired isn't the worst thing. I sort of like it."

Things were sure different for her, Jordan thought. If he stopped working, by the weekend he'd be living in a refrigerator box with a pet rat and a bottle to piss in.

"How do you like the sushi? The food is good. I've always liked the Tokyo Inn. It's not loud like some of the other sushi bars," he said.

"I used to come here often but I stopped."

"Why?"

Daphne smiled oddly.

"My old boyfriend liked to come here when we were in town. He reserved one of the private rooms, and I brought along my girlfriend. I had to go to the bathroom. When I returned, they were making love, right there on the floor just like in *Genji.*"

"What did you do?"

"I backed out and shut the sliding door," she said.

Jordan didn't know what to think. She told the story as though she was talking about the weather.

"You must have been pretty mad."

"I was hurt, but he had great powers of suggestion, mind control, something. I think he was a hypnotist. He said I shouldn't get upset. Jealousy is stupid and a waste. The expression of love in whatever form is what life's about."

"You believed him?"

"Yes, at first. But later I became depressed. I thought I was flawed for being jealous and undeserving of his affection. I thought about my soul a lot. No matter what happened to me, at least I could keep that pure."

"What's his name?"

"I don't like to say it."

"You don't have to."

"It's Frank," she said, almost in a whisper.

"How old were you?"

"Sixteen."

"How old was he?"

"Thirty something."

"I would have killed him," Jordan said flatly.

"What?"

"See, if I had a daughter and someone like that decided he was going to spend his time dogging her, I'd wait until he came home and drive my car over him a few times."

She grimaced. Then she was silent for a long moment.

"My mother tried talking to him. At that time I was so mesmerized that my girlfriend smuggled me back to my parents, knowing that if I saw him again, I'd be as pathetic as before. My parents immediately sent me to stay with relatives in England. Somehow, he found out about the plan, and he was determined to follow me and tried to badger my mother into giving him my number. She tried to talk him into leaving me alone. She tried threatening him with the police, but by the time she finished talking to him, she was almost seduced into

75

telling him to come pick me up. She hung up and refused to answer the phone for weeks."

"What happened to him?"

"Last I heard he was in New York getting rich and fat."

"Maybe he'll have a heart attack."

"You must trust me or something to tell all this," Jordan said.

"I do . . ."

Suddenly awkward, she paused as if she were searching for the next word.

"A walk on the beach?" she asked, almost blurting it out.

"Yeah, sounds great." Jordan took out a few twenties to pay the bill but she shoved the bills into his shirt pocket.

"Let me," she said, and put her own bills onto the table.

At the beach the night was warm. After reaching the pier, they continued on to where the big waves broke against and over the seawall. She stopped and pointed to the waves.

"The water is glowing."

Every time a wave broke, the foam glowed bright green.

"I think they call that bioluminescence, something to do with plankton. It only happens once or twice a year. I think I read that in *Believe or Not!*"

So near, but he couldn't bring himself to touch her. Farther up behind the pier, the tide was out. They hopped down and walked to where boats were stranded in sand, near the wooden seawall. Jordan again tried to find the nerve to kiss her, sensing she waited patiently for him to do something.

"May I kiss you?" he finally heard himself asking in a voice that seemed unlike his own.

Without hesitation she kissed him. A perfect intimacy, in a

perfect setting, holding onto her, wanting to remember: her taste, the thickness of her hair as he ran his hands though it. Afterward, they walked hand in hand to the car. He wasn't letting go of her now, touching her hair, brushing her arm as they drove to her house. There, she quietly led him through the dark house to the guest room behind the stairwell. She turned on the light and stretched out on the narrow bed. Again he froze, incapable of moving a muscle, but she took control, rubbing his shoulders, guiding him down next to her. There she kissed him again, passionately. Arousal finally thawed him. He ran his hands along her body, but they were on the wrong page. He realized she had drifted off. Now what? What to do, watch her sleep or . . . he leaned over and kissed her again. She woke.

"You'd better go. I'd love for you to stay but I've been home only three months. I don't want to disappoint my parents so soon."

Jordan sighed. "Last thing I want to do is get you in trouble," he said, without conviction.

She walked him through the jungle-like living room to the glass door and waved good-bye. He watched her retreat up the stairs to the security of the second floor.

Only people with money could feel comfortable with the whole world able to look into their living room like it was some human aquarium, he thought. He drove home feeling elated at how well things had gone, but there was something else, an uneasiness. Afraid of a brutal landing, he didn't want to fall any harder than he already had.

Christmas Eve anticipation of late-evening drives, weekend rendezvous at Pismo Beach Motel where they'd be too deep under the covers to find daylight or see a wave crashing against the surf, died pretty suddenly when Daphne didn't show up for class. The five students who did come to class must have seen the disappointment in his eyes, or maybe they couldn't because as they discussed *The Makioka Sisters* he craned his neck at all the footsteps echoing in from the hallway.

He dismissed them early and hurried to the car and drove like a fool to Hope Ranch, flooring it along those narrow roads until he reached her driveway. Now what? Roar on up to the house and rap on that stupid glass door until she opened it? Then he could shout like a madman, "Where were you!" or "One date and you're ditching class?" Jordan gave up. He returned home and tried calling her but the phone rang unanswered. Maybe he read the date all wrong; what he thought of as the beginning of something serious meant nothing to her. Finally, it came time to meet Ned in the gym for a b-ball pickup game, but he had to struggle to resist calling Daphne, or taking another drive to spy on her house. Through an act of nerve-jarring self-discipline, he pulled himself from the phone. He'd wait for class to meet again.

Thursday. Two juniors and three seniors but no Daphne. This time he held class to the bitter end, and moped through office hours wondering just how silly he was to get himself in such a situation. No judgment, that was clear.

Daphne was nothing but bad news. How could he expect things to work out? It was like she was from some weird foreign country, where they did everything ass-backward—give play to the guy teaching your class, then blow him off. He should have been more wary, not silly and love struck right from the get-go.

"Excuse me," he heard from the hallway. The last thing he needed was a student showing up to discuss a fucking essay, but then he looked up to see Trisha in a short skirt, smiling awkwardly.

"Hi, Jordan," she said, uncomfortably at the threshold of the office.

He pulled a chair out for her.

"I've been meaning to call you but things have gotten really busy."

"I know this isn't any of my business but I heard you've found a new girlfriend."

"Who told you that?"

"So, you're not seeing anyone?"

"No, nothing serious."

Trisha brightened at his reassurance.

"I want to invite you to dinner," she said, shyly.

"That sounds great but I'll take you. Make amends for being so flaky."

Trisha kissed him good-bye. As he slid his arms around her, he remembered how good she felt.

"How about tonight?"

"Great!" she said.

After another brief kiss she hurried to class.

Jordan arrived home to find an expensive flower arrangement looking seriously out of place in the clutter of the kitchen table. The flowers were exotically unfamiliar, vibrant and intensely fragrant. Beside one particularly phallic-looking pistil he came across the card: "Sorry I missed class. Family crisis—will explain soon."

Ned as usual was on the steps of their run-down bungalow, lost in the daily sketching of the Taco Bell across Milpas; one in an unlimited series, he liked to say.

"Ned!"

Ned ignored him and continued with the nearly completed sketch.

"You saw Daphne?"

Ned waved him away.

"I'm making art here. Talk to me later."

"Ned!"

"Man, you just gotta know now?"

"Yeah, now."

Ned sighed and put down his pad.

"She just dropped those flowers off, gave me a big sloppy blow job, and took off."

Jordan laughed and clapped his hands together.

"So, what did you think? She looks good, huh?"

"I see why you're so hot on her. She's got some great legs, showing them off in that short-ass skirt, I mean, if you like thin legs. Yeah, she's fine. Looks a little like Sade. Plus, she's real pleasant. Not stuck-up like I thought she'd be."

"Yeah, she's not stuck-up. Flaky, yeah. Stuck-up, no."

"What? She blew another class?"

"Yeah."

"Oh, she's making sweet with you for that good grade without doing the work. See, that's why you're not supposed to be dating students."

"Ned, I'm not giving her a grade. It's pass, or no credit."

"Still, a pass is something."

"Yeah, right. It's easy giving advice."

"It's easy to see she's playing you."

"She's not playing me, she's just . . . I don't know."

"Good. She wants you to call, and you can figure that shit out."

"I'll call her, but not tonight."

"What's tonight?"

"I'm seeing Trisha."

"Cool, show some resolve."

Jordan shrugged and returned to the house. He sat at the kitchen table, looking at the flowers. No one had given him flowers before, and it made him feel uncomfortable. He liked them, and he liked that she would do something so unexpected, but he wasn't tempted to call. Daphne, as beautiful and fascinating as she was, had put a scare into him. Just like when he lost contol of the Triumph; he needed to get his feet back under him. Hell, he hadn't even been seeing her long, and already he knew he was in love, but being in love with somebody shouldn't make you feel your world was on the verge of exploding.

CHAPTER 7

This wasn't how she wanted the afternoon to go. To her surprise, her dad wanted everybody home to discuss family business. She was on time and her mother wasn't; because of that she sat trapped in the family room having to endure watching him puff an unlit pipe as he gazed through the sliding-glass doors at the shrub-covered hills of the San Marcos Pass. Wordlessly, that's the word that summed him up and drove her nuts. If only he had said just a little about why this was so important. They just sat in silence. Finally, the sound of the door opening; her mom arrived a half-hour late, wearing a new, brilliant teal-colored waistcoat.

"About time!" her father said, with refreshing emotion.

Trisha, also irritated with her mother's habitual lateness,

couldn't help admiring how she ignored her father's tone, smiled sweetly, and slid onto the sofa.

"I called Rob and Mark about this, and now I'm letting you know," he began. "I'm resigning from General Electric."

Now, this was something Trisha didn't want to hear.

"Resigning? I thought you were looking forward to returning to work," Lady Bell said, with concern.

"They didn't give me the promotion."

Lady Bell looked momentarily stricken before bouncing back to cheerfulness. Trisha could barely conceal her anger; what she thought would be a path straight to law school now seemed convoluted.

84

"They didn't?" Mrs. Bell asked.

"They gave the vice presidency to some white jackass. Why is it that when whites pick their own, it's fair, and if we get picked, it's affirmative action?"

After a long silence, nobody answered, but Lady Bell brightened.

"Retirement is good. We'll be able to travel."

"I'm suing."

"Suing?"

"Yes. Sue! It's racism, plain and simple."

How tense he is, even answering the simplest question, Trisha thought.

"Do we have the money for that?"

"Of course we do. If you stop shopping every day of the week."

"I'll get a job," Trisha said, before she knew she was going to say it.

He nodded his response.

"We'll have to cut back to weather this," he said, disappearing into the den.

Trisha sat near the pool feeling bitter and overwhelmed. It wasn't just her father retiring, but something else with him. She just wanted out, like her brothers got out. Leave it to Lady Bell and Pie to figure out what was up.

The phone rang, and in a moment Pie appeared at the kitchen door, gesturing at the phone in her hand like it was something filthy.

"It's for you. It's that David," Pie said, frowning.

Trisha shook her head; she didn't want to talk to him. Pie smiled evilly as she turned around and hung the phone up.

David had started coming by and hanging around the pool like he was staking a claim, and she was getting tired of it. It was just a joke. David was gay, and she had suspected it for a while; he just thought she was too naive to put it together. He had some master plan that only a man with a gigantic ego would consider; he needed it all, wife and kids and, of course, when he got around to it, a boyfriend on the side. That she couldn't figure out, David's need to appear straight. He was good for one thing, though—making Jordan jealous. David pissed him off in a big way. She needed Jordan in her life right now more than ever, but everything was complicated with him. Could she sleep with him? That was the biggest complication; unless she could give him that, she was sure their relationship was dead and he'd end up in the arms of another woman.

*   *   *

"Law school—it's what I've wanted to do as long as I can remember, but now who knows?" Trisha said to Jordan, as he served her pad thai at the restaurant on Milpas.

"It'll work out, but I wouldn't let this stop you. Even if he can't afford to send you, you could get support. Look at me, ten years of government support," Jordan said.

Government support? Why should her father's support suddenly be eroded, by what, his desire to resign, retire, sue? He was too young to retire.

"Look, if he sues and wins, you'll be rich. GE has deep pockets."

"But why now? The one thing he said is never explain or complain, just get the job done. So, I got the grades, the LSAT scores, and now I'm supposed to put it all on hold?"

"Something must have pushed him."

"It's always been like that. He's worked all his life with white boys who have every advantage but brains. I remember going to his office and seeing a chalkboard covered in equations. My father spent the day solving problems for the engineers. He won so many awards, but they overlooked him time and time again."

"I think you need to talk to him. Find out what he's thinking."

Trisha shook her head.

"He doesn't communicate well. He's like those engineers he instructs; words make them nervous. You know, I started off as an engineering major, did all the course work, but I gave it up. I like words; they calm me. Numbers don't. They make me think of pencils and paper and sweating through tests."

They ate silently until Jordan slipped his hand over hers and laughed.

"You're so serious. It'll work out. I stopped looking for support from my father soon as I was out of diapers."

Trisha sighed.

"I know it just seems like I'm complaining. It's just unfair that my brothers stayed in school for years, bumming around. Me, I'm in school for the minimum number of years, and I get shortchanged."

"You can't dwell on it. You'll just get bitter."

"So I won't be bitter. I'll put myself together, but you have to tell me about this new woman. Don't deny it. You were seen."

Jordan sighed, covering his face with his hands.

"I don't have a new woman. What is this, a black spy network?"

"Yes. It's the sista syndicate."

"All I did was have coffee with a friend. We're not seeing each other. That's all that's going on."

"So, this friend happens to be a beautiful white girl with curly hair."

"She's not white."

"She's not? That's news to me. Regardless, she dresses like she lives in San Francisco or New York and has money to spend. My spy said you kissed her good-bye."

"Kissed her good-bye? That's a lie."

Trisha's eyes flashed.

"Listen. I know you can see anybody you want. Plus, I don't know where we're headed anyway."

"Trisha, I like you a lot. You're very different from any woman I've met."

"You just better be a good friend to me."

"I am."

"Then be honest. If you've fallen in love with this Daphne, just tell me."

Jordan sighed.

"Listen, I might have had a little interest in her, but it's over."

"Well, I guess I have to believe you."

Trisha paused. She knew he was lying but she didn't want to fight with him.

"It's a beautiful night. Do you feel like a drive?" she said.

He laughed.

"I guess I'm out of the doghouse."

"That depends on how far you drive."

"Pismo Beach, that's thirty miles. Is that far enough?"

"We might never get back," she said, and kissed him.

Jordan stopped at his house to pick up a contact case and condoms. He rushed into the living room where Ned rested on the couch watching a *Star Trek* rerun and listening to Les Nubians. Captain Kirk mouthed to soulful French singing.

"Going to Pismo with Trisha," he said over his shoulder, as he hurriedly grabbed the few things he needed.

"Damn, you on a roll. Fine sister yesterday, fine sister today."

"Yeah, I'm a pimp."

"You dog. Don't let her see the flowers. She's gonna know Daphne sent them."

"She's waiting in the car. How's she gonna know?" But as he said the words, Trisha opened the screen door and walked into the kitchen. Almost instantly she noticed the flowers on the book-covered kitchen table.

"Oh, those are nice and expensive. Who are they for?"

"Ned . . ." Jordan said, nervously.

"Ned gets flowers?"

Ned shrugged, poker-faced.

"He's doing a still life," Jordan said, but Trisha ignored him.

"Who is she, Ned? You've met somebody?"

"It's for that woman I don't know yet. I buy fresh flowers each week just in case I meet her."

"You're not serious," Trisha said.

"Oh, yes I am," Ned replied.

"We'd better go," Jordan said, leading Trisha outside, with Ned waving a little too enthusiastically behind them.

Trisha slid close to Jordan as he drove the Triumph north up the 101. Once they cleared the eucalyptus groves, the ocean unfurled, a calm, silvery seascape paralleling the highway. They reached Pismo Beach in thirty-five minutes but it wasn't fast enough for Trisha. That engine sounded like a dozen blow-dryers pointed at her ears. Even with the engine off she heard a dull roaring.

Jordan hurried into the motel lobby. Alone, Trisha leaned against a wall to avoid the cold wind blowing in from the ocean. She didn't feel the same confidence she had felt earlier. What if she did it and it didn't keep him? What if he ran straight back to this new woman?

He returned after a few minutes with the keys and wrapped his arms around her.

"Man, it's cold tonight," he said as he led her to the room. He opened the door to a room with furniture so old it was hip again. Jordan rolled about on the bed.

"I love sleeping in motels, hotels, whatever. I get sleepy just thinking about sleeping."

Trisha busily hung the few clothes from her suitcase and arranged her things.

"We're gonna be here until morning, and you're hanging clothes?"

"I always hang clothes. I can't sleep if I don't." In truth, she was just glad to have something to do. Finally, she headed for the bathroom to change. Jordan poured the wine and set out the condoms. He had a couple of glasses while the minutes stretched to a half hour, just enough time to start thinking about deflowering, devirginizing, busting the cherry; whatever it was called. It was too nerve-racking. Coming in third or fourth was best; too much pressure taking that first giant step for mankind. With Mary there was negative pressure; he was hard from the moment they were within shouting distance. Trisha, now this meant something. It meant he drank half the bottle of wine before she opened the bathroom door.

She came out, backlit nicely, in a Chinese silk robe, open along the front to reveal a red teddy. Despair hit him square in the groin. This was a mistake. She curled into bed next to him. He handed her a glass of wine from which she took only the briefest of sips; then she turned out the light.

"I think we should just relax. You know, rest. I'm a little burned out from the drive," he said.

Jordan paused, thinking of something else to say, but she kissed him. If he was going to do the deed, he figured the safest course would be to make this the longest foreplay of his life. How did "To His Coy Mistress" go? . . . "Two hundred years to adore each breast" . . . Yeah, he'd make her explode with desire, and maybe he'd relax long enough to get an erection. Ten minutes later he was fumbling with a rubber.

"Wait a minute—do you know . . ."

Here it comes like clockwork.

"I guess you know I'm a virgin."

"Yeah, I never suspected."

"What do you think about waiting?"

"Sure, wait. Why not? We have all night, the morning . . ."

"Until we're married."

Cold water crashed against the modest embers of his desire.

"Now, that could be awhile."

"Would you be mad at me if we waited?"

"Well, I . . ."

That was it. She crawled on top of him, but her eagerness seemed forced.

"You don't have to do this," he said.

"You don't want to? You want to wait?"

"I mean, waiting is fine if you want to wait."

"You don't mind?"

Her small breasts looked perfect, inches from his mouth. How was he supposed to show restraint?

"I don't know. I mean, we're different. I need things, but I respect you—you know, your beliefs."

His hands slipped to her hips.

"I'm using a diaphragm. It's my first time trying it out," she said, as though she had made a joke.

"Let's just take this slow," he said, with new resolve, and slid her off him.

"You're not disappointed?" she said, on her back, looking up at him.

He looked down at her on the verge of panic, wishing he had had the foresight to have put virgins out of his mind altogether. He should have worn a T-shirt that said something like "No virgins accepted here," or "Will not deflower!" He patted her shoulder, and tried to ignore that blood red teddy barely restraining her hips and breasts.

"I'm willing to wait," he said, and took a deep breath. Trisha kissed him on the cheek and whispered, "Thank you for being so patient."

Somehow that was enough. Not getting laid wasn't the end of the world; not if the weight of the world rested on a cherry.

In the morning, Jordan woke to a fully dressed Trisha, sitting across from him at the room's desk reading *Pismo Today!*

"Ready for breakfast?"

"No, I think I need to get back home."

"So soon?"

"Yes."

Jordan sighed, and dressed without looking at Trisha.

"Breakfast really means that much to you?" Trisha finally asked.

"Breakfast means a whole lot to me."

"Okay, then. I have time for breakfast."

"Cool," Jordan said, grinning.

Farmer Boy Restaurant was on the other side of the pier but it was so crowded that only a few counter seats were open.

They waited in the still foggy morning air for a table to free up and were surprised to see another black couple exiting the restaurant in high spirits.

"Look, more colored folk. Maybe this is the hangout," Jordan said. After hearing his name called, he happily led the way into the bustling Farmer Boy. It annoyed Trisha how cheerful he was.

"Jordan, we need to talk about last night."

Jordan tensed to her words.

"Last night?"

"Yeah."

"What happened last night?"

"You know what happened."

"We slept. I thought that's what you wanted to do."

"Yes, but . . ."

"But what?"

"You didn't even try."

Jordan sighed.

"Listen, I don't force women into doing something they feel uncomfortable about."

Trisha looked away from him.

"I thought maybe you didn't like me, or weren't attracted to me."

Jordan sighed.

"I like you. That's why I didn't try. . . . It didn't matter that much to me."

"So, you're saying that if you didn't like me, you would have tried harder?"

He paused, trapped.

"These women you sleep with, you don't like them?"

"It's not really like that."

"What's it like, then?"

"I like you a lot."

"Like? You have sex with women you don't like. You have respect for me, probably because I haven't slept with you."

"Now, that's bullshit."

"Is that what happened to the new girl? She gave it up and that was that?"

Jordan stood up, yanked some bills from his wallet, dropped them on the table, and walked out.

Trisha had never seen him so mad.

Outside, she saw him far down the road, walking quickly on the shoulder of the highway.

"Jordan! Jordan!" she called.

She waited a half hour before Jordan returned, acting calm as though nothing had happened.

"What's with this running off?"

Jordan shook his head.

"You don't want to talk about what I mean to you, or what this other woman meant to you. Some people would say that makes you a dog."

"You really don't understand men. I'm not a dog. I don't try to dog women. Sometimes things get ugly and there's nothing you can do about that. It's the way it is."

Trisha sat quietly, wondering how she could have spent the night with him.

As they drove south, the fogginess cleared, and the ocean was choppy and blue. On their left the rolling hillsides were green, and the many dark oak and walnut trees were in bloom, verdant leaves against black branches. Jordan slipped in a CD,

94

and the car filled with Al Green. She wanted to be angry with him for the entire ride back to Santa Barbara, but she couldn't. Everything was so perfect; the empty highway stretching like a long ribbon before them, the sharpness of the morning air, the smell of the ocean. They passed a few dilapidated farmhouses that looked sufficiently melancholy, but what caught Trisha's interest was a boarded-up roadside café with an "Eat" sign high enough for even the most unobservant driver to see. Obviously, it didn't attract enough attention to keep the business going. The café was made to resemble a train car with portal-shaped windows and a railroad-crossing sign above the entrance; it looked as sad as she felt. She wondered if it was for sale. Maybe she could buy it and she could retreat from life, running a roadside diner. What would the locals say? "That black girl's diner can't be beat." Locals, tourists, and maybe even some cowboys, if they weren't total racists, would come by for good Southern cooking. The restaurant would become a local institution because Pie would train all the cooks. Trisha would make more than enough money to buy an old farmhouse and restore it to its former glory. There, she'd live alone with yard dogs and house cats, content to read fat Trollope novels. She'd spend the years in spinsterhood because this rat, Jordan, couldn't be honest.

"So, why do you feel so comfortable in Santa Barbara?" she asked, over the dull roar of the engine.

"Don't you? It's beautiful. The ocean next to the mountains. No smog. People leave me alone. It's safe."

"But I was born here. I'm used to being the only black person around. I have my family, some friends. I know how to live in this world. For you it's got to be different."

"Hey, I made my own life here. Everybody has to figure it out for themselves. It's everything I need at this point. What should I do, find some corporate job, be a suit? I spend mornings at a café reading, having coffee, walking to the ocean. I get paid to talk about books. It's a good life."

Trisha wanted to respond but her thoughts became jumbled. Her life was so utterly unlike his; she didn't feel like she could judge him, but she did.

"Are you running from Los Angeles, from black people? It's where you come from. Don't you feel like you don't belong here?"

"What?"

"Only since I got to college do I feel like I truly belong. It was nice when I was little, but eventually I started to understand; my father was the first black on the Santa Barbara board of education. Even here in this quaint tourist town, we received death threats. I had a policeman driving me to elementary school and parking in front of our house. I know this place, the good and the bad. I don't see how you can come up here and spend a couple of years and feel like Santa Barbara is it."

"Eight years."

"Whatever. You still think you fit in."

"You act like there's a correct way for me to be living."

"I think it's more than that. I think you're running from yourself. You want to be someone else."

The Triumph accelerated sharply. Ninety easily, but if that's how he hoped to change the subject, she wasn't intimidated.

"You don't understand. I've lived a little bit. I dealt with this before. A woman checks you out and doesn't like your prospects. Let me tell you, it's worse back in the big city. I always had a job. Once I worked at a fish market over on Fairfax. I made some decent money for a high school student; I had a sweet little Mustang and all the new sneakers I needed. One day I had to pull a morning shift because the owner was sick. I knew I wouldn't be able to get home to shower. I scrubbed up at work and rushed to school for an exam in my English class. Somebody got a whiff of me, you know, smelling of fish. I get called 'Fish Sauce' for the rest of the year. Everybody was calling me 'Fish Sauce'; scrubs, girls I was trying to get over with, my so-called friends from Baldwin Hills who didn't need to work at a fish market. You want to know what I learned from that? Do what you please 'cause people will do their best to try to shoot you down."

Trisha shook her head. What the hell was he talking about?

"Jordan, I respect you. I'm not criticizing your job, or how you're living your life."

"Then what exactly are you criticizing?"

Finally, he slowed to negotiate the sharp turns to her house. There, Trisha bolted from the car, but she turned to meet his eyes.

"You're not being honest with me," she said.

"I'm through with you picking on me, sitting in judgment of me. I know what you're mad at. You think of me as some race traitor because I like living in a beautiful city anybody would want to live in. Your father made that decision; do you give him the grief you're giving me?"

"No."

"Okay . . ." He finally looked at her, his eyes showing anger, but more hurt.

"Call me?" she asked, as he put the car in reverse and swung around to coast downhill. She wanted another "okay," but he said nothing. Instead, he waved weakly and rolled away to freedom.

She didn't want to face her parents or anyone else. Before she could decide what to do, her mother and Pie arrived.

Through the window she could see Lady Bell crying and heard Pie's gravelly voice, "Tell the girl."

"Bad news, Trish. Daddy's in the hospital."

"What?! What's wrong?"

"He has to rest," Lady Bell said.

"The man's gone and let himself have a nervous breakdown," Pie said, harshly.

Right as Trisha's knees buckled, Pie's strong arm grabbed her around the waist.

Inside the house, Trisha noticed the stacks of books almost to the ceiling, blocking the kitchen and hallway doors.

"The bookcases were too difficult to move so he moved the books," Lady Bell said.

"All night that man's been acting like a nut trying to build a wall of books," Pie said.

"Dad?"

"Oh, yes. It was quite a scene. I've never seen him like that."

Her mother's forced cheeriness finally cracked. Tears streaked her face faster than she could wipe them away.

"Aw, yeah. Then he got out that golf club and chased us."

"Chased you?" Trisha asked.

"Well, he was trying to protect us," Lady Bell said. "From the voices he's hearing."

"Protect us? That man just wanted to run us around the house like some chickens. Lucky we got it from him before the police came. Coulda got ugly."

"All this happened last night?" Trisha asked, following Pie and Lady Bell as they inspected each room of the house, assessing damage. Chairs stacked on couches, couches pushed against doorways; almost every doorway had some kind of blockade even if it was no more than television trays piled high with ancient *Reader's Digests*.

"This is where he was holed up," Pie said. "In the master bedroom." 99

"Mom, I left him last night and he seemed okay, just tired. I made him a burger before I left for Michelle's."

Pie, though in her seventies, pushed aside the couch blocking the way to the family room and rearranged it in its normal position facing out toward the pool. Lady Bell smiled gratefully and sat down and gestured for Trisha to do the same.

"Your father has been on medication for depression for the last year."

"You didn't tell me?"

"He made me promise not to tell you or your brothers. He hoped to protect you. He hears voices. He thinks we're in danger."

"In danger from what?"

Lady Bell sighed. "He thinks we have enemies. People, Caucasians, who want to . . ."

"Lynch y'all," Pie added, as she went about straightening the room.

"The doctor worried that your father might become more depressed, but we didn't think he'd be like this."

"Great," Trisha said, putting her face in her hands.

"Y'all ready to get back to the hospital? Mr. Bell is gonna need his things."

"Right. I have to pack a bag for your father."

"A bag? How long is he supposed to be in the hospital?"

"'Long as the Lord wants him there," Pie said.

Lady Bell began to cry again but she slipped away to pack before Trisha noticed. Trisha found herself doing the same but her tears turned to sobs. Pie came over and sat with her.

"Trish, don't worry. Your daddy's gonna be fine. That man is just tired. That's all that it is. He just needs to rest."

Trisha pulled herself together long enough to nod.

Trisha watched her mother enter the hospital room, hoping she didn't have to follow. She had no idea of what to expect, and since she wasn't given a hint by Pie or her mother, she expected the worse. She wanted to sit next to Pie and wait the whole thing out, but Pie frowned her disapproval.

"Go on. You ain't gonna let your mama do all that grieving by herself, are you?"

Reluctantly, Trisha entered the room. She saw her mother sitting gingerly on the edge of the bed, holding her father's hand. Trisha could barely bring herself to look at him. It was obvious that he was heavily sedated, but she noticed the straps to hold him down.

"Daddy?" she said.

He continued lying there, sphinxlike. She wanted to leave as fast as she could, because looking at him was making her panic. Even sleeping, his face looked as rigid as raw iron. He was incapable of relaxing even with all kinds of tranquilizers pumping into him.

"Trish," he finally said.

"Dad?"

"Trisha," he repeated in a surprisingly strong voice. "I want you to . . ."

She waited for him to complete his sentence, but he became even more rigid, gritting his teeth; then a slight shaking started, and it grew stronger.

Her mother ran out for help.

"It's okay. . . ." he said, his voice falling to a whisper. "Listen . . . protect yourself. These people want to destroy us. Your mother doesn't know the danger. Watch out for these white people. They'll destroy you. . . ." His voice trailed off.

Then Lady Bell returned with a nurse. The nurse didn't look surprised.

"He's been like this, slipping in and out of consciousness, becoming aggressive and then withdrawing."

With those words, Trisha returned to the waiting room. Pie was there to hold her as she cried her eyes out.

101

CHAPTER 8

Jordan and Ned arrived on State Street after a two-mile jog from the sad little shack on Milpas. A run downtown on a warm afternoon guaranteed serious girl-watching. Maybe they'd make it to the wharf for cheap fried-catfish sandwiches, but if they ended up eating at the Italian deli on Cota, that was cool too.

"You gonna miss all this," Jordan said.

Ned shrugged. "Yeah, another beautiful day in paradise, but I'll get over it."

"Soon as it starts to snow your ass will be driving straight back to Santa Barbara."

"I don't think so. D.C. got a whole lot of sistas and I got a whole lot of catching up to do."

"Man, you could find a woman here," Jordan said.

"Like you? All the women you mess with are too high

maintenance for me—like that Daphne; I thought you were through with her."

Jordan shook his head.

"I thought I was. She came to class last week, and it's back on. I just looked at her and I knew I was sprung. I mean, it's bad. If she wanted the keys to the Triumph, I'd go gas it up and get it waxed before I'd hand her the pink slip."

"As much as you love that silly little sports car, you must be in love."

"Yeah, I'm gone."

"Don't lie, you like it."

"I'm just hanging in there, waiting for the wrong turn, hoping I have time enough to throw myself clear before the big crash and burn."

"You should stop with the stupid car metaphors, but I'm gonna give you one: If you don't watch out, you gonna have a head on-collision with a broken heart."

Jordan laughed, then stopped and turned at the sound of an alarm ringing faintly in the distance. A crowd gathered at the jewelry shop next to the entrance of the faded pastels of the El Paseo courtyard. Ned hung back, but Jordan headed into the crowd spilling from the sidewalk into the street. Minutes later he returned, shaking his head.

"Look at this! Basketball players facedown on the ground."

"Basketball players?" Ned repeated. Ned followed Jordan, maneuvering until he had a clear view of three very tall black men in expensive sweatsuits, handcuffed, facedown on the cold concrete.

The shortest of the basketball players called to the police, but it was hard to understand him because he had to speak with half his face pressed against concrete.

"We're the Harlem Globetrotters!" the guy said, over the sirens of approaching patrol cars. The policemen ignored him, milling about, talking among themselves.

"Now, that's fucked up. That is the Globetrotters. They're playing on campus tonight," Ned said.

"They'll let them go now," Jordan said.

Ned was backing away, retreating to the edge of the crowd and waving for Jordan to follow.

"Come on, we've got to go," Ned said, harshly, pulling at Jordan's arm.

At first he didn't understand, but then a patrol car slowed as they crossed the street onto Cañon Perdido.

He understood. Black men were in season.

"Don't turn around. That cop is checking us out!"

Jordan couldn't help glancing over his shoulder at the blond cop in the patrol car. It hit a U-turn and rolled on them. The cop bolted from the car with both hands on his gun.

"Hands on your heads. Turn around. Get against the car! Spread them!"

Almost instantly they were swarmed by more police, springing out of nowhere. A beefy cop handcuffed them; first Jordan, then Ned.

"Ned?" he said, turning him around, appraising him. "Wait a minute! You're Ned in my watercolor class."

"Yeah, you're Bob. You do those watercolors of Ellwood Beach. This is my friend, Jordan Davis. He teaches at the university."

"Oh, yeah. You mentioned him. You teach creative writing, right?"

"Yeah, I do. Sometimes."

The cop shrugged. "Okay, obviously we have a problem. Three black guys robbed a jewelry store."

"Those guys you got on the ground are the Globetrotters. They play on campus tonight," Ned said.

"That's what they said. Man, shit is going to fly."

He turned away to talk to the other officers and reappeared after a few minutes.

"It's out of my hands; we're going to have to take you to the station," he said, avoiding their eyes. He opened the door of his patrol car and carefully guided them into the backseat.

"Yeah, some paradise," Ned said.

"This is ridiculous," Jordan said. "He knows you."

"Yeah, he does, but we're all suspects. Those Globetrotters got to be thinking Santa Barbara knows how to treat a black man."

They sat in the patrol car long enough for a fairly large group of gawkers to gather across the street to watch them. They stared right back.

"They probably think we killed somebody. We're celebrities," Jordan said.

"Fuck celebrity," Ned said.

Bob returned and helped them out of the backseat and uncuffed them.

"Sorry about the inconvenience."

"Hey, don't mention it. See you in class," Ned said.

They crossed State Street, scattering onlookers, mostly kids hanging out in front of McDonald's. They headed back to the relative security of Milpas to wait out the craziness. Ned laughed, breaking the silence of the walk.

"Too bad we didn't have a real asshole arrest us. A little beating and we might have got a big settlement."

"Yeah, or a nice funeral," Jordan said.

The entrance of the Pub was jammed, but that didn't slow Daphne from jockeying for position to reach the doorman. Jordan was reluctant to follow. He couldn't help noticing that the crowd, pressing hard to enter the last dance club open at one in the morning, was overwhelmingly male. When Jordan trailed too far behind, Daphne reached for his hand to keep him close. The burly doorman who looked more like a bouncer, shirtless and dressed in red leather overalls, had a disconcerting, inch-long screw through his nose. He gave Daphne a curious once-over, collected the cover, and let them through.

Inside, the booming bass line made conversation impossible, and dancing was almost as impossible; too many people squirreling around for a bit of room to move. Daphne still maneuvered forward, around the men lingering at the edge of the dance floor. One ran his hands along her sides; Daphne ignored the gesture and shoved on. Miraculously, she found a tiny corner of unoccupied space and leaned close, shouting into Jordan's ear, "Do you feel uncomfortable here?"

He shook his head but it was an obvious lie. Grimly nodding, he was too unnerved to even glance at the men dancing almost directly in front of him. Maybe she was testing him, he thought. Seeing if he was a homophobe.

He was beyond uncomfortable. Suffering was more like it.

"Care for a beer?"

He nodded, and Daphne took off for the bar. From the start she was gone too long. He felt very, very awkward alone; frightened someone would chat him up or discover he was some hetro tourist, slumming in a gay club, soaking up the local color. Now that his eyes had adjusted to the lighting, he could see that there were some women out there, but then he noticed men kissing against the wall. In spite of trying not to, he found himself staring and felt guilty about his curiosity. He thought about Jake in *The Sun Also Rises,* wanting to bash the gay guys coming to the Bal. Remembering the scene made him want to laugh; there he was sympathizing with a homophobic, racist white man because he was worried somebody might hit on him. Fuck Hemingway. He decided to find Daphne, but there she was, coming to the rescue with beers in hand. She looked delighted.

"I saw one of my professors at the bar."

She pointed nonchalantly to a tall, balding man at the counter having a beer. The professor caught their stares. Daphne waved to him as if to break the ice. Startled, the professor abruptly turned away and lost himself in the humanity.

"I didn't mean to scare him off. He's my religious studies instructor, and I do believe he's married with kids."

Jordan strained to hear her over the music.

"Maybe he was just having a beer."

"And looking for love in all the wrong places?" she replied, laughing.

He shrugged. He couldn't understand what she said but her attention was elsewhere. She watched the dance floor with hawkish intensity. Jordan was content to have Daphne pressed close against him. With her there, the red strobes firing every other second, and thunderous, discordant music booming against the skin, the smoke, the bitter odors were perfect in a hellish kind of way.

"This is the promised land!" he shouted over the din to Daphne. "And you are my people. Robert Cohn is too."

"You're a fool," she said, and kissed him fiercely.

"You're right, I'm a fool."

He wished that they were already back to her almost empty apartment, just a bed and a desk and her equally spartan refrigerator, nothing but mustard and coffee and mineral water. About the only other thing in the apartment was all the sand in her bed. He remembered her lying there naked in that gritty bed, looking vulnerable as if she had just been born.

"Is that one of your friends?" she asked, nudging him.

"Huh, who?"

She pointed to a black man on the dance floor. He had his back to Jordan. Jordan shrugged.

"Because he looked at you like he knows you."

"Oh," Jordan said.

The sweltering room became even more of an oven; Daphne's blouse clung like wet tissue, and her breasts gleamed alluringly. He kissed her neck and slid his hands to her breasts, releasing them from her flimsy bra. She squeezed against him and whispered something that he couldn't make out. Jordan and Daphne were both soaked with sweat, kissing hungrily. She pulled away, breaking the spell.

"Look, your friend is coming over."

Jordan saw him, but at first his face didn't register. Then

he knew him—David. Coolly nodding to Daphne, David held his hand out for Jordan to shake.

"Hello, Jordan, enjoying the heat?" David said, shouting over the music.

"Oh yeah."

"It gets worse. Are you going to introduce me to your friend, or are you trying to hide her?"

What an asshole, Jordan thought. Bet he can't wait to run to Trisha with tales: Yeah, Trisha! I saw him with that girl he's so in love with, feeding her a mile of tongue!

Grudgingly, Jordan made the introductions.

"David, this is Daphne; Daphne, David."

David shook her hand.

"You are too lovely to be with Jordan. Would you two like to join us?"

Daphne smiled shyly but shook her head. Jordan didn't bother to respond.

"Well, it's been wonderful. I'll tell Trisha I ran into you."

He finally left. Jordan slipped into a Trisha-inspired funk. Why did hurting Trisha's feelings bother him so much? He couldn't help but hurt her. It was so easy. She had the values of some Victorian heroine: prideful, proper, and virginal.

"What's wrong? Since David left you've been staring off into space. I'm not standing in the way of something, am I?"

He grimaced.

"Forget it. Let's dance."

She entwined her hand with his, and they found a bit of space on the dance floor so confining that they hardly had room to move. Jordan enjoyed feeling Daphne writhing against him, but he wondered if David was checking them out, and the enjoyment fled like air from a balloon.

"You keep looking for someone. David, maybe? Why don't you ask him to dance?"

Before he could become annoyed, she slipped her fingers around his, and kissed his cheek, running her lips to his ear.

"Look to the far right," she said. Jordan glanced in that direction expecting to see another professor or maybe a preacher, but he caught a glimpse of David dancing with a well-dressed blond guy.

"What do you make of that?" Jordan asked.

Daphne shrugged.

"What's to make of it? Two guys dancing at a gay club."

"I mean, do you think he's straight?"

"What do you think?"

Jordan turned to see another man standing behind David's partner. This guy was a big man, probably a weight lifter. He locked the blond guy's arms in a half-nelson. David continued to dance with his restrained partner, pretty much crotch to crotch.

"Still wondering if he's straight?"

Jordan shook his head.

They watched the threesome dance, doing a kind of three-headed tango.

"They're very good together. Maybe they practice," she said.

"Yeah, maybe so."

Jordan wasn't really listening to her. Instead he was thinking of just how naive Trisha was. Couldn't she see that he was gay? And what about David, didn't he know that he could see him over there doing the Freak with a lumberjack and some preppie guy? David was busted but he didn't seem to care. What did he want with Trisha anyway? Did he need a wife or a girlfriend for cover? Maybe he was considering a run for the senate and figured he needed a wife for the campaign flyer. The song ended, and the dance floor cleared, as people searched for air and cooler temperatures. But what was this engagement thing about? Was he just trying to mess with her mind?

"I'll be right back," he said, gesturing to the rest rooms.

It took a few minutes to locate David outside in the enclosed patio area, huddled close, sharing a cigarette with the blond guy.

"David, excuse me. Let's talk, if you got a minute?"

At first David smiled at him, taking a moment too long to respond.

"Sure, I have a minute."

Jordan hoped that David would excuse himself from his friend, but the friend lingered near them.

"Look, I know this isn't any of my business, but Trisha mentioned that you two are engaged."

David raised an eyebrow and stepped away from his friend, who looked curious. Jordan was glad to have David look uncomfortable if only for a passing moment.

"Oh, she did? I thought she wanted to keep it a secret for another month."

"I don't mean to butt in, but I'm concerned for her. I mean you're here with . . ."

Suddenly, Jordan was at a loss for words.

"Gay men? Some of whom happen to be my friends?"

"Okay, but what I'm saying is . . ."

"Am I gay? Is that what you want to know?"

Jordan shook his head, embarrassed.

"If I were, what would it matter? I asked her to marry me because she makes me happy, and I believe I can make her happy. Marriage is something I take seriously, faithfulness, all of it. I wouldn't do anything to hurt her."

Jordan had nothing else to say.

"What about you? Trisha cares for you, and she says you care for her, but you have a thing for pretty girls. Where did you meet this one?"

"Hey . . . that's not how it is. Trisha is the one who . . ."

"And she is pretty. I mean, so many black men who decide to date out of their race choose such dogs. You've found an ex-otic, and Trisha even mentioned that she's rich. You can see that. She reeks of it. She'll improve you."

Jordan was impressed. David had a tongue like a god-damn viper.

"Look, David, I'm not the one we're talking about. If you care about her, you need to be honest."

"This is where I came in," David replied, glancing at his friend waiting patiently for his return.

"See, Jordan, I don't owe you an explanation, nor do I need your friendly advice."

David walked away, leaving Jordan standing there stupidly.

Jordan returned to Daphne and led her from the club without a word.

Over the roar of the engine and the wind, Daphne's voice in-terrupted the silence.

"I'm sorry I brought you. I didn't know you'd have such a bad reaction."

"It's not that. David is dating a friend of mine. Actually, he's engaged to her."

"Does she know he's gay?"

"I don't think he thinks she needs to know. She's a virgin and doesn't know much about men."

Daphne laughed.

"So, is it your job to save her?"

"No, I'm not saying that."

"Then why are you so worried about their relationship? She'll discover he's not interested, sooner or later . . . if she cares."

He couldn't find a place to park near her studio apartment at the top of the Riviera.

"Don't worry about parking. I have to get up at seven to go to the farmer's market with my mother. Remember, tomorrow you're to come by for dinner. My parents are looking forward to meeting you."

They kissed warmly, and Jordan waited until she was safely in her apartment before coasting downhill.

He figured the house would be quiet at three in the morning, but all the lights were blazing and the windows were wide open.

There was Ned packing his belongings for the long trip back to civilization.

Jordan walked in and startled Ned, nearly causing him to drop his milk crate of belongings.

"What's up?" Jordan asked.

"My life. Getting my life in order."

"So you're really going to do it?"

"Yeah, time for a change."

"What day are you heading out?"

"Tomorrow, man. I told you that. If I linger around too long, I may change my mind."

"You can't go tomorrow. What's the rush? It's almost summer. The beach . . . you love the beach."

"You just don't want to have to find another roommate."

"Art says he wants in. I just think you ought to hang out a little longer and don't rush things."

Ned laughed.

"You oughta come with me. We could get a great place much cheaper than here. Shit, we each could have a floor in a cool townhouse. All kinds of sisters looking for degreed young men like ourselves."

Jordan shrugged.

"Sorry, man, you know I'm down with California. Hey, you remember David?"

"The Negro with the phony English accent, yeah."

Jordan waited for Ned's full attention. Ned complied and looked up from sorting through a mound of CDs.

"And?"

"I saw him at the Pub."

"Damn, Jordan, you went to that gay bar?"

"I was with Daphne."

"Yeah, that explains it. Is she a transexual? If she is, I got to get me one. What about David? You saw him there getting personal with some jocks?"

"Well, yeah. He was there with a couple of men doing a slow grind."

"I thought you said he was engaged to Trisha. That doesn't

sound like what you do when you about to be married to a woman."

"Naw, it doesn't."

"Well, it ain't your business."

"That's what Daphne says."

"Unless, you still trying to beat David out for Trisha."

Jordan shrugged nervously.

"If that's what you trying to do then you oughta be happy, 'cause this David ain't even in the game."

"Yeah. I know."

"But then you back where you started out, deciding who you gonna be with."

"Yeah, I know . . . I got to crash," he said, and headed for the bedroom.

Asleep as soon as his head hit the pillow, he dreamed of the steering wheel of the Triumph coming off in his hand, and plunging headlong into the Pacific.

The next morning on his way to the university, Jordan tried not to think about Trisha, but he couldn't help it; she was just that naive not to see what was right there in her face. Jordan couldn't stop from exiting and driving to San Antonio Creek Road. What to do now? he thought as he sat idling at the base of their driveway. Was he going to be the carrier of tales? "Look, Trisha, I don't know how to tell you this, but your fiancé was dancing cheek to cheek with not one man, but two. Don't ask me how I know, I just do. And if he mentions anything about me and Daphne, he's lying."

Just then he saw Lady Bell gunning the SUV down the driveway, waving hurriedly as she made the sharp turn on to the main road. Then, realizing it was Jordan, she reversed and pulled alongside him.

"Good morning, Jordan. Trisha said you'd be coming by," she smiled, made a quick turn, and sped away.

Jordan rang the bell hoping to see Trisha, but Pie's grim face startled him.

"You ring that bell like you never had a bell to ring."

"Sorry, I didn't mean to."

Pie waved for him to follow, and he did, staying a respectful distance behind her broad back and curly, jet-black wig that she wore at a rakish angle. She led him to the master bedroom where Trisha sat on her parents' bed with stacks of paperwork before her.

117

"This boy wants to see you. I hope he can see you busy," Pie said, cutting her eyes at him.

"It's okay, Pie. I have a few minutes."

Pie grumbled something and left the room. Trisha kept at her work, barely glancing in his direction.

"How are you doing? Is everything okay?"

"I'm okay," she said.

"What's with the paperwork so early in the morning?"

"My father is in the hospital. He had a nervous breakdown."

Jordan paused for a minute, wondering if he should ask anything more. Trisha seemed on the verge of crying.

"That's horrible . . . you must be feeling . . . horrible."

"I don't have time to feel horrible. His insurance is screwed up, something to do with him retiring."

"How's your mother taking it?"

Trisha laughed bitterly.

"She spends all her time at the hospital. I spend all my time sorting papers and making phone calls. I hate sounding selfish but I graduate next month. I expected to be happy at least for a day. Now everything's falling apart."

Jordan leaned against the wall, thinking he should have called first.

"So, you've come to tell me about the nightclub? David said you'd be by."

Jordan shrugged. David had beaten him to the punch.

"Well, yes . . . I thought you should know."

Trisha finally smiled.

118

"I'm glad you're so concerned for me, but I'm a big girl."

"What did David say? Did he explain?"

"He said you were there with a very pretty girl. Daffy, he said, but I knew he meant Daphne."

"Yeah, we were there, but David was . . ."

"I know, dancing with two men. He said you'd get all excited about that."

"So that's not a big deal to you?"

Trisha slipped a rubber band around some of the envelopes and began sorting through a fresh stack of dog-eared letters. He waited anxiously for her to say something, show some outrage, anger, or irritation.

"Why do you think I'm so stupid? I know David very well."

"That's it? You didn't have him explain himself?"

"Usually, I don't demand that my friends explain themselves."

"But he's not just a friend. You're engaged to him and he's gay as tomorrow!" Jordan shouted.

Trisha laughed.

"Don't get so excited and get Pie coming in here with a skillet to bust you in the head with."

"Trisha, I don't think you have a clue of what you're doing," he said, louder than he had wanted to.

A sharp knock on the door, and there was Pie glowering at Jordan.

"What's this boy being so loud for?"

"It's okay, Pie. We're just having a loud conversation."

"A conversation? Y'all yelling."

"I'd better go," Jordan said, and turned to leave.

"Thanks for coming by," Trisha said, "and checking on me."

Jordan nodded, and as fast as he could, he walked away, but not before Pie's, "Don't go stomping through the house!"

As soon as Jordan was gone, Pie turned and gave Trisha a big grin.

"You got that boy so jealous he can't see straight."

Trisha barely looked up from the stacks of bills surrounding her.

"Huh, Pie? I didn't hear you."

Pie straightened her apron and headed back to the kitchen.

"Don't you worry; that boy don't know how stuck he is on you," Pie said, as she shut the door.

Jordan blew off his office hours, and returned home and spent the rest of the day working on his thesis. Mostly he spent the time trying to make sense of years of notes that no longer seemed insightful or even meaningful—it was actually sort of pleasant working. "Kind of Blue" crept down weakly from a San Luis Obispo radio station, lessening the bitter boredom of reading a stack of academic journals. He forced himself through a paragraph of prose so stultifying that it had to be in some language that only idiots could or would want to read. His attention, like the jazz station, flitted in and out. He watched traffic race up and down busy Milpas, counting the cars that ran the red light. He watched the teenagers on their way to the Taco Bell as he discarded dead and useless research into the wastepaper basket. Yeah, he'd finish that thesis, and then he'd submit it and get on with his life. Somebody might even find "Jazz: Influence and Fluency in Contemporary American Literature" worth reading, but he had to finish it first. He had no choice; with just a little imagination he could see the unemployment line snaking all the way to his dusty bedroom. Time to get real about finding a serious teaching gig that paid for dental care and all that job security he heard so much about. His mind flitted again; Daphne and tonight's dinner, what was that going to amount to? It must be getting serious, but he was probably just blowing it out of proportion; her parents probably wanted to see what kind of black man she was sleeping with.

Normally, he wasn't in his room at the computer this late in the afternoon. He stretched out on the bed and shut his eyes; dinner wasn't for another couple of hours. He hoped he'd wake in time, but if he didn't, well . . .

"Wake up."

He opened his eyes to see Daphne in a flimsy dress smiling at him.

"Your hair is wet," Jordan said, sitting up.

"I was swimming at Boys' Beach."

"The nude beach?"

"Yes, it was kind of ugly. This hairy fat man, with a thing

so large it looked deformed, waited at the shore for me to come out, and no matter how far I swam, he followed me."

"What did you do?"

"I waited 'til some guys came along, and then I sprinted by him."

Usually, Jordan could hold a conversation even if he wanted to jump on Daphne's bones, but this particular battle was already lost; the thin material of her soaked dress could barely restrain her erect nipples. She stretched out next to him on the bed, and immediately he lifted the damp dress and kissed the curve of her hips.

"Daphne, I uh . . ."

"Jordan, the window."

"Yeah, right."

Jordan closed the blinds and turned to see Daphne peel off the wet dress. He couldn't get out of his pants fast enough, but eager as he was, he tried to slow the process down. He wanted to commit her to memory: her eyes, her legs, her breasts, her mouth. She guided him in, and he worried he'd come at once, but skillfully Daphne stopped the chain reaction, slowing the motion until he could move inside her without exploding. He whispered, "I love you, I love you." He wanted her so much that if he died right there, it wouldn't have mattered. He held her tighter, breathing in the air she exhaled, inhaling everything about Daphne.

Afterward, they rested on his narrow bed, but Jordan's mind raced, devising ways—marriage, kidnapping, drugs—to have her again and again, afraid to think of living his life away from her.

She met his eyes, looking as though she would reassure him

121

and put him at ease that she felt the same overwhelming love.
She looked away.

His heart sank.

"I should go. I need to help with dinner," she said.

He watched her wiggle into the still wet dress and leave in
such haste she had to come back for her shoes. She didn't say
good-bye, and even though he'd see her again shortly, it bothered him, like a window opened to an impending storm.

Jordan arrived at Daphne's on time but wondered if he should
drive home to find a tie. He wore a jacket, white shirt, khakis,
and penny loafers. Anybody could see he was no wild man,
more like Denzel than Tupac. Her parents would see that he
was just an instructor . . . who happened to be freaking their
daughter . . . while she was still a student in his class.

With that, he sat back down to rethink the whole thing.
He was sure that this dinner would be awkward and weird,
maybe even a disaster.

He arrived at that hated glass oval door and waited uncomfortably like a trapped bug for someone to answer the doorbell.

Daphne ran down the stairs in a red sarong and with her
hair pulled back and braided. Seeing her so soon after making
love made him feel as though it hadn't happened. He wanted
proof. Before she could say a word, he kissed her.

"I missed you," he said.

"It's been so long," she said with a laugh, and led him to
the sunroom behind the kitchen. Her mother stood up from
the table to greet him, as did her father. He looked to be much
older than the mother, with a narrow red face and sharp teeth
like the Renfield character in *Dracula*.

"Glad you could make it," he said.

Jordan shook his hand. Mr. Daniels gestured for Jordan to sit. The table had a centerpiece of fruit and cheese, and next to it, two bottles of wine. Jordan imagined the old man—"More flies, Master!"—begging for bugs.

"Red?" Mr. Daniels asked. "The red is very good."

Jordan nodded, wanting to laugh.

"So, you teach at the university?"

"Yes. I teach a Japanese lit class under the supervision of the provost of the college."

"Daphne goes on about how much she enjoys your class," Mrs. Daniels said. Her tone was pleasant and her smile seemed genuine. Jordan relaxed a bit.

"She's a wonderful student and about the only one who keeps up with the reading. The *Tale of Genji* is pretty tough going in places."

"I'm surprised to hear that Daphne is applying herself," Mr. Daniels said.

"Do you speak Japanese?" Mrs. Daniels asked.

Jordan shrugged. "Well, I've had four years of Japanese, but I barely can ask, 'Where's the rest room?' I'm language-challenged."

"You've lived in Santa Barbara long?" Mrs. Daniels asked, to restart the conversation.

"For almost ten years."

"So, you like it here?" she continued.

"Yes, I'd like to make Santa Barbara my permanent home."

"Really?" said Daphne. "I couldn't spend the rest of my life in this city. . . . It's claustrophobic," she said.

He was surprised that she would disagree with him so quickly in front of her parents.

"I like it here," Jordan said. "It doesn't have to be claustrophobic."

Daphne sighed.

"You have to make your life wherever you are. I find Santa Barbara interesting, and I've lived here all my life," Mrs. Daniels said.

"Maybe our daughter needs more excitement," Mr. Daniels said. "Though you would think she had had enough at this point."

Jordan hadn't even had much of a drink or an appetizer, and already the evening was on the verge of blowing up.

"So, Daphne," Mr. Daniels said jeeringly, "where would you like to live?"

"I liked New Zealand," Daphne replied.

For no good reason, Jordan commented, "In New Zealand, sheep outnumber people ten to one."

"Still, even with all those sheep, Daphne managed to make a time of it there, too," Mr. Daniels said.

Mrs. Daniels obviously wanted to lighten up the conversation. She patted her husband's hand and smiled apologetically at Jordan.

"You were arrested and thrown out of the country," Mr. Daniels said.

Jordan glanced at Mrs. Daniels, who looked worried. Daphne eyed her father grimly. Mr. Daniels sipped at his water, ignoring her stare. Daphne picked up a teacup and gripped it so tightly that Jordan was sure she would hurl it at Mr. Daniels' head.

"My family can be difficult," Mrs. Daniels said pleasantly.

"What family isn't?" Jordan said.

"Here, here," Mr. Daniels said, and poured everyone another glass of wine.

"Len, help me with the chicken," said Mrs. Daniels. Without a word her husband stood and dutifully followed his wife into the kitchen.

"Now comes the scolding," Daphne said, smirking.

"Is everything going to be okay?" Jordan asked.

"Of course. He can be very pleasant when he's under control. He probably missed taking his Zoloft."

Jordan still felt uncomfortable.

"My family has hope for me."

"Hope?" Jordan asked.

"Hope that things work out for me, that I don't disappoint them. They treat me like I'm capable of anything; suicide, joining a cult. I used to think maybe they were right, that I couldn't hold it together, but being adopted gives me hope; that's the only reason I'm sure I won't go insane."

Jordan waited for her to go on, but she didn't. Instead, she smiled at him. He tried to contain his curiosity, but he didn't do a good job.

"Don't tell me you're surprised? I thought we talked about this," she finally said. "I'm not nearly so pink as they are."

He shrugged.

"Father was English, and Mother was a mixed-race South African woman. I was adopted at four into a life of affluence and what else: cocktail parties, fund-raisers, depression, family viciousness."

"Did you ever meet your biological parents?"

"No. I used to think that I could find them, that they were out there somewhere, waiting for me. Maybe that's why I started running away."

Mr. and Mrs. Daniels returned with a roasted chicken and a plate of steamed vegetables. It didn't help Jordan find his lost appetite, but it was just as well. Hard to make a good impression when your mouth is full.

As soon as everyone was served, Mr. Daniels started in as if he was continuing a conversation. "You must know that anyone trying to understand this family has to be prepared, because we live on the verge."

126

"The verge of what?" Jordan asked.

"The verge of disaster," he said with a labored, straight face.

Jordan wished he was driving and not Daphne. It had seemed a good idea to drop his car off and drive with her, but now she was barely hitting the brakes as she negotiated the hills. How much farther to her apartment? Jordan wondered, weighing whether he should suggest that she slow down, but thankfully he didn't have to. She turned into an oddly angled parking space, cut the engine, and burst from the car, running for her apartment up the hillside.

Jordan thought for a minute that she must have really had to go. He waited a minute, then five, before knocking, but the door was open, and he found her under the covers shaking.

"Daphne?"

She didn't respond. He took a few steps toward her and she pulled the covers higher.

"Should I go?"

Finally, in a strained voice she said no.

"What is it?"

"Panic."

"You're having a panic attack?"

"It happens when I spend too much time with my family."

The covers inched down. He sat on the edge of the bed and held her still shaking hand.

"Have you been to a doctor? Can't he give you something for anxiety?"

She sighed as though she had heard this too many times.

"Of course, if I wanted it."

"You don't?"

"I have absolutely no interest in that kind of treatment. I don't want to change myself."

He started to reply but she pressed her finger against his lips.

"Let's go to sleep."

"Sure," he said. He got out of his clothes and slid next to her, ignoring the grit of her sandy bed. They made love, and he tried to reassure her as they did that he would protect her, that she didn't have to be afraid of anything. He looked down at her face, at her lips; everything about her was precious to him. He held back, wanting to show her how much he loved her, how much he wanted her to share in what she made him feel. Finally, he lost himself, whatever he was thinking; Daphne grasped him around the face, kissing him between half-gasped words.

"Don't hold back; I want you to give it to me. Give it all to me," she said.

Like he had a choice.

*　　　*　　　*

Morning light: the bare white room seemed cloudy as if he had dreamed her next to him—cold feet against his, the scent of her hair. He was almost fully awake but fought it, delaying it as long as he could. He knew once they were awake they'd part, and he wasn't ready for that.

Boom!

They both bolted upright to the sound of someone pounding on the door. She gestured for him to be quiet.

"Daphne! Goddamn it, Daphne! I know you're in there. I know you're home!"

Jordan's heart pounded as hard as that lunatic outside beat the door. Daphne didn't seem alarmed. She looked almost indifferent.

"Open the damn door!"

Jordan struggled into his pants, no way was he going to get shot down like a dog, in his boxers. He ran into her tiny kitchen looking for something to defend himself and Daphne with, but all he could find was a teapot and a butter knife. Hearing the chain being taken off the door, he rushed in and saw Daphne in a robe talking to a balding, powerfully built white man in an expensive suit.

"I didn't know you had company," he said, pleasantly.

Daphne seemed at ease, even pleased to see this man who had been pounding at her door moments before.

"Frank Willis," he said, extending his hand, which Jordan ignored.

"What's with pounding on the door?" Jordan demanded, feeling more ridiculous by the moment, trying to look tough with a teapot in his hand.

"I should go. Having a working vacation, as they say."

Frank gave Daphne a warm embrace and walked out, closing the door behind him.

Jordan couldn't bring himself to look at Daphne. He dressed, ignoring her eyes as she lingered by the door, arms folded as though the man was still there. She could explain but Jordan wouldn't ask; too much mystery with her already.

"Look, I'm gonna be going."

"Jordan."

"Yeah?"

"You have every right to know what's going on."

"You think so?" he said, bitterly.

She sat on the edge of the bed as he opened the door to leave.

"I can explain. Give me time."

"You don't have to. Really. I'll see you around."

As he walked out of the apartment, he glanced back. Her face was vacant of emotion. He knew he should have been pissed off, enraged, but something was so wrong with her. He was more mad at himself; he should have seen it coming, but still he got run down like some blind, deaf, and dumb idiot.

He pulled into his driveway to the sight of Ned's fully loaded van, packed to the roof with suitcases and boxes. Somehow he had forgotten Ned was leaving today. He felt doubly sick to his stomach; losing a woman and a best friend on the same day.

He walked up the rickety steps of the hovel and through the screen door could see Ned and Art sitting down to a feast at the sad little kitchen table, so weak it wasn't holding up

129

well under the weight of the spread, a whole Mexican-style roasted chicken, watermelon, tamales, a mound of chocolate chip cookies, and a big pitcher of lemonade—all Ned's favorites.

"Hey, J! Come on in before we knock this all out," Ned said.

"Yeah, Trisha brought a feast."

"Trisha! Did she ask for me? What did you say?"

"I said you were . . . out doing Daphne. Naw, man, I said you had to run an errand and you'd be right back. You lucked out; she had to go home for a second."

Jordan sighed and slumped into a chair, but then they heard the roar of Trisha's SUV.

"You in trouble now. She's gonna smell the woman on you," Art said.

"Women have that sixth sense," Ned said, "and heightened powers of smell."

Jordan bolted from the table and ran to the bathroom. There, he locked himself in and tore off his clothes, tossing his jacket, shirt, and pants into a hamper. He showered vigorously to rid himself of any lingering Daphne, found a pair of stale running shorts and a T-shirt, and stepped out to meet Trisha, who was seated next to Art and across from Ned, looking entertained and content with their company. In tight black jeans and French-cut T-shirt she looked as good as the last time he saw her.

"Hi, Trisha," Jordan said, feeling suddenly guilty. Maybe that was part of her charm, her ability to make him feel guilt.

"Hello, Jordan," she said, still with a bit of frost in her voice.

"Are you going to have breakfast?" she asked. "How was your run?"

"Run?"

"How far did you run?"

"Too far. The run was rough."

"You look like you showered. You always shower and put your running clothes back on?"

Jordan sighed, rolling his eyes.

"No."

"He's just too cheap to buy enough fresh underwear," Ned said.

After breakfast they stood around Ned's van watching him make a final check, then after the farewell embrace, Trisha returned with a colorfully wrapped box for Ned.

"I hope you can use it," she said, gesturing for Ned to open it. Inside he found a multipurpose emergency flashlight.

"It's very powerful. The salesman said don't look directly at the light because it could cause eye damage."

"Is that a selling point?" Jordan asked, but Trisha ignored him.

Ned looked unsure of how to respond to the gift. Trisha gave Ned a farewell kiss.

"You two should quit playing and set a wedding date," Ned said. "See, I can say anything I want now that I'm out. It's like being on your deathbed or something."

Trisha and Jordan looked at each other uncomfortably.

Ned pulled his van into the street and waved at them as he drove off.

"Y'all live long and prosper. I'm gonna miss you."

"Call collect. We want to know how you doing on the

131

road!" Jordan shouted, but Ned was halfway down the street.

"I'm gonna miss him," Art said, holding up one of Ned's many sketchings of Taco Bell.

"Me too," Jordan said, walking to the street and staring after the van.

"Jordan, are you okay?" Trisha asked, but Jordan kept his distance, not wanting to explain his tears.

CHAPTER 9

Trisha remembered writing a paper on the history of psychiatric hospitals. This hospital had to be "Bedlam Lite," with its sturdy furniture and cheery tile and big-screen television; more a rec room in a college dorm if it wasn't for the dozen or so glassy-eyed zombies watching television with rapt attention. Other than the one dark-haired, mushroom-pale man walking in tight circles angrily muttering, "Those bastards, liars, kill them all!" the room was calm and more sedate than she had any hope it would be.

Her father waited on the couch farthest from the psychiatric patients. She tried to look at ease as she approached him, but it disturbed her how he stared so fixedly at the ground. Only when she reached out for him did he notice her, and then it was with alarm. After slow recognition, he reached to embrace Trisha with unsteady eagerness.

"Hi, Daddy," she said, avoiding his eyes. At least he looked much better this time; much more animated than last week.

"Good to see you," he said, warmly.

"We miss you, Daddy," Trisha said.

"As you probably expect, I can't wait to go home."

"Yes, I'd want to go home too."

"How's your mother holding up?"

"She's doing great."

"I hope this move isn't too much for everybody. It must be overwhelming."

134

"No, it's going okay. But I never imagined how much we have."

"That's your mother. She's a damn pack rat."

The "pack rat" irritated Trisha. She decided to bring up a subject she knew would sting him.

"Your lawyer called."

He leaned forward and gestured for silence. Then he stood and escorted her to one of the unopenable windows.

"The lawyer is one of them. Whatever he says, don't listen."

"Mr. Johnson?"

"Yes! He's in on it. That's why I'm here. Too much is at stake. He's in the plot against me."

"Dad . . ."

"That's why they have me in here. I've made plans. I'm not going to be an easy victim."

Alarmed, Trisha remembered her father purchasing a shotgun last year.

He gestured for her to listen.

"Ask to speak to my doctor. Find out what you can."

"Dad, I . . ."

"Do it!" he said, and walked away so quickly she didn't have time to respond. He disappeared down the hall leaving her to wonder if he'd return. He didn't. She sat there watching the patients watch television until she got the nerve to ask for his doctor. At the nurse's desk she had to wait for the nurse, a heavy woman with a quick frown, to finish what seemed to be a very long personal call.

"May I speak to Dr. Seto?"

"I'll see if he's available," the nurse said, more gruff by the minute.

"The doctor is coming out to speak to you. Please have a seat."

After a forty-five-minute wait he finally appeared, an athletic Asian man who had the walk of a surfer. Trisha stood to meet him.

"Miss Bell?"

"Yes."

"Dr. Seto," he said, as they shook hands. "I'm glad you're here. We need to discuss your father's release."

"His release?"

"Yes. He's responding well to his medication. We have him on a low dose of an antipsychotic drug. He's making marked progress."

"Really?" Trisha said, slumping against the wall. "You know, I've never found out exactly what's wrong with my father."

The doctor glanced at the chart in his hands.

"This isn't an exact science, but we know he's suffering

from paranoid delusions, and he's been deeply depressed for quite some time."

"And you believe he's better?"

"Well, he'll never be better in the sense of something like this never happening to him in the first place. For the rest of his life, he'll hear voices. Nothing can change that, but with medication and supervision hopefully he'll be able to manage."

"Doctor, what if he's still experiencing paranoid delusions?"

"Unfortunately, he probably is. It's a matter of management. I talked to your father at length. He's extremely intelligent and self-aware. I think he's a good candidate for release."

"Well, I'll explain all this to my mother and she'll get back to you." Trisha rushed to the elevators praying she wouldn't see her father standing by the window, searching for enemies, obsessed with his family's survival.

Home, she found her mother in the master bedroom, folding clothes.

"Oh, you're back. I forgot to give you his clean clothes for the week."

"Don't worry about it. He's coming home soon, or at least the doctor thinks he should."

"It's a blessing," Lady Bell replied.

"Do you think he's ready? At the hospital he said some pretty crazy things."

Lady Bell cleared space on the couch for them to sit.

"I haven't noticed."

"Maybe he isn't taking the medication," Trisha said.

Lady Bell frowned and straightened the clasp holding her long hair into a tight bun.

"Your father has always been a little paranoid."

"I thought this was the first time he had a nervous breakdown."

"No. His work has always been hard on him. He doesn't talk about it but it was easy to see. He was the only black person to reach that high in management at General Electric, but they overworked him and wouldn't promote him like the others. Things became a little easier but it never stopped grinding away. He wanted you to have the best; the best education, the best neighborhoods, and he sacrificed for it."

Sacrificed his sanity, Trisha thought.

"Mom, we need to do something about that shotgun he has."

Lady Bell paused, considering Trisha's remark.

"We need to get that gun out of here before he comes home," Trisha added.

"He'll be very upset."

"He'll just have to be upset," Trisha said.

"Okay, you handle it."

Trisha knew she'd get stuck with the responsibility.

"Maybe Jordan will know what to do," Trisha said.

The last few weeks she and Jordan were easing back into seeing more of each other, and he seemed to want to see even more of her. While Jordan made it clear that he wasn't seeing Daphne, she didn't really believe him. More than likely they had some falling out, and it was only a matter of time before they'd get back together. Jordan seemed too interested in talking about

David, and that made her suspect that maybe he was just jealous. That's what she wanted him to be, but if that was the basis of his coming around, that wasn't what she wanted either.

In truth, she didn't know what she wanted.

She drove the few miles to Jordan's. There, she saw his Triumph in the driveway, but she didn't pull up behind him. Instead, she parked on the street. Now she knew what she wanted, at least for the moment—to catch him cold; see if he wasn't keeping his word about Daphne. She imagined Daphne stepping into the shower with Jordan, wild soapy sex ensuing.

She knocked on the door and felt her stomach tense at the sound of someone approaching. It was Art.

"Hey, Trisha, Jordan's coming right back. Come on in."

She followed him into the dusty living room. Art was a nice guy but he had weird taste in clothes. His jacket was the brightest yellow she had ever seen on a guy—bumblebee yellow—and it seemed even brighter in contrast to his brown skin.

"Where did you find that jacket?"

"The thrift store on State. I think it's part of a uniform for a hamburger stand."

Art pointed to the cursive "Stanley" above his chest.

"I just bought this huge sombrero. Ugly chic, baby, and this is ugly chic."

"Yes, it is." Trisha said, as she slipped by him and through the living room into Jordan's bedroom.

She had liked Jordan's small, neat bedrom, but she no longer felt comfortable in it. Jordan had probably slept with Daphne on this bed. Of course he had. He slept with her there, and who knows where else. Daphne could easily give him what she couldn't, but Trisha wasn't going to sleep with him to keep him. It wasn't just because she was a Christian; she wasn't made that way, it meant too much to her.

She heard someone coming toward the bedroom. Jordan was startled to see her, just as she had hoped; and just as she had hoped, he was alone.

"Hey, I was going to call you."

"Jordan, I need your help."

"Sure, what is it?"

"I need you to take my father's shotgun to the police station."

Jordan laughed.

"You want me to go to a police station with your father's shotgun? Okay, a black man shows up with a shotgun and says he wants to give it to a policeman. Yeah, that'll work."

"I called. The police say it's okay."

"That's easy for you to say. Nobody's going to shoot you and call it a mistake."

Trisha sighed. "They said put the gun in a paper bag."

"Now, that'll calm everybody when some cop notices I got a shotgun in a garbage bag. I guess you didn't see *Terminator?*"

"Well, you could keep it here."

Jordan shook his head.

"No, that's not an option. This is one black man who hates guns. Don't like to have them near me."

"So, you'll do it?"

"Drop the gun off at the police station?"

Trisha did her best to look like she needed this done more than anything in the world.

"Okay, but let me ask you this. How come you just don't take it yourself?"

She laughed. "Because I asked you to do it."

"Well, that explains it. I'll come by and pick it up . . . soon."

"It's in the car."

Jordan sighed.

"You want me to do it right now?"

"Yes."

"Great. You drive, in case something goes wrong. You can watch me make the evening news."

140

During the short drive to the police station on Figueroa, Jordan continued to glance into the backseat at the shotgun Trisha had wrapped like a Christmas present, neat and well taped.

"That gun should be in the trunk. What if the police stop us? They'll think we're some kind of black Bonnie and Clyde."

"You worry too much."

Jordan shook his head.

"Rich girl, you don't know. That's what I like about you. Raised in Santa Barbara, might as well have been Mars."

Trisha stopped in front of the steps of the police station.

"You're in the red. I guess you don't want me to reflect too long on this."

Trisha nodded.

"Okay, if this makes up for . . ."

"For dumping me for Daphne? No, it doesn't. . . ."

Jordan sighed and unlocked the door.

"Okay, here goes," he said, without moving.

"It's probably best you get it over with."

"I'm doing this because you don't think your father should have a gun?"

"Yes, he doesn't need one now that he thinks 'they' are out to get him."

"Who's 'they'?"

"'They' are whoever he thinks 'they' are."

Jordan sighed deeply, and turned around to reach for the shotgun in the backseat.

"Okay, this is where I get cut down in my prime," he said, and opened the car door and stepped out holding the shotgun against his leg in a halfhearted attempt to conceal it.

"Now we'll see just how vigilant the Santa Barbara police are."

Trisha watched him walk up the stairs to the station like he was going to his own execution.

This shouldn't take long, she thought, but as the minutes slipped away and Jordan didn't return, she wondered if something had gone wrong. She was about ready to go on into the police station when she saw Jordan sprinting down the steps like he was running for his life.

"Go! Go!" he shouted, as he jumped into the car.

Trisha tore out but slowed when she noticed Jordan grinning like a pumpkin.

"You dog!"

"I was waiting on a claim ticket and the cop started talking about people dropping off guns."

"And . . ."

"He says that it happens all the time. Family trouble and other family members want the guns out of the house, but he

141

said people don't want to think about how easy it is to get another gun."

"Great," Trisha said. "That's what I needed to hear. That's all the trouble I need."

"Anyway, I'm glad we took care of that. When's your father coming home?"

"Any day now."

Trisha shook her head, dreading more and more her father's imminent return home. She hardly noticed arriving at Jordan's place on Milpas.

"You want to come in?" Jordan asked. "Maybe we could get some lunch."

"Thanks, but I need to be home to help my mother."

"Maybe later on tonight."

"Jordan, I need to ask you another favor."

Jordan sighed, shrugging.

"What, you want me to wash your dog or something?"

"No, I want to meet Daphne."

Jordan's face fell slack with surprise.

"Why in the world would you want to meet Daphne? I told you I'm not seeing her. She's got a boyfriend."

"Yes, I know, so it shouldn't be a problem."

"What shouldn't be a problem?"

"Arranging for us to meet."

Jordan walked in loopy circles around the car shaking his head.

"I can't believe you're insisting on seeing her. You don't believe me when I say I'm not seeing her?"

Trisha took a moment to reply.

"I believe you, but I need to ask her a question."

"What question is that?"

"It's not for you. It's for her."

"Trisha, I can't possibly call her. I haven't talked to her in weeks. She's . . . she's back with her old boyfriend."

"Oh."

"See, I told you. Everything is different."

"Jordan . . . you want to know what's happening with David."

"Yeah, but . . ."

"Well, I want to know Daphne. I mean, if you want us to be closer. Isn't that what you said? Since we couldn't get any closer, we needed more space."

143

Jordan shook his head.

"I didn't say anything like that. I didn't say anything. It's what you said. You're putting words in my mouth."

"Admit it. It's because I'm a virgin."

Jordan sighed, and looked at her through the window as though it was the first time he saw her.

"Trisha, I don't care if you're a virgin. That's a decision you made, and it's important to you. I'm different from you. I have another set of values."

"What's that? Dating women who sleep with you, but break your heart?"

"Trisha . . ." Jordan walked all the way to the porch and back.

"Just ask her. I'm not psychotic."

Again, Jordan shook his head in disbelief.

"I'm not calling her."

"Jordan . . ."

She gave him that on-the-verge-of-tears look, and he crumbled.

"Okay, I have a compromise. Be right back."

Jordan ran into the house and returned with a phone book and handed it to her.

"Look it up. The Daniels family—Hope Ranch Road."

"Me?"

"You can ask her yourself."

At first Trisha wouldn't look at the number, but Jordan held the phone book out right under her nose.

"I could copy it for you," he said.

"No, that's okay. I have a phone book at home."

"So, you're going to do this?"

She waved good-bye and left him there in the driveway, shaking his head.

Home, Trisha unlocked the door and hurried inside hoping no one else would be there. She needed to call Daphne before she lost her nerve. Good, no sign of Mom. Better to speak to your nemesis alone. She used the phone in the kitchen and while dialing looked out at the pool and beyond the pool, to the ocean at the horizon. All of this she'd be losing now that Dad was retiring. Daphne didn't have these problems, born with a silver spoon embedded so deep in her throat she didn't have problems. She probably never had to work at fitting in. If she were as pretty as she had heard, men had a way of ignoring a little coffee in the cream. Trisha had been plagued by Daphnes—rich, beautiful white girls—her entire life. This Daphne wasn't white, but she was close enough; one of those charming octoroons, those Jennifer Beals, Mariah Carey types who don't live in a black world unless they want to. It would probably be easier if she were just another airhead blond having an adventure messing around with Jordan. Daphne probably was discovering her roots with Jordan, whatever those might be.

She dialed the number.

"Girl, your mama's at the hospital picking your daddy up."

"Pie!"

"Yeah, that's my name."

Pie walked to the sink, looking more grim-faced than usual as she filled a plastic bucket with sudsy water.

"Something wrong with Dad?"

"Oh, no. That doctor say that Mr. Bell is fine enough to come home and be with y'all."

Pie had on her housecleaning uniform, starched white even down to her white rubber soles.

"Ya know, since y'all moving into that apartment and gonna be renting this out, this gotta be presentable. Otherwise, only people gonna want to rent it is gonna be pigs."

"Pie, you shouldn't be cleaning. Mom is going to hire a crew to do what we don't finish."

Trisha watched as Pie wrung out the sponges and wiped down the wooden blinds around the sliding-glass doors like she had a grudge against them.

"Something wrong, Pie?"

"Naw, nothing wrong . . . 'cept I can't believe you moving down the hill."

"Dad's plan makes sense. We don't need this big house, and since he's retiring, that'll cut expenses way down. And I'll be away at the law school."

Pie's mouth contorted to a sneer.

"Yeah, but y'all still don't got enough money for you to be going to law school. It ain't fair to you. Mr. Bell should have thought about it before he up and retired like that."

"Pie, I think he's retiring because of his health."

"Ain't nothing wrong with your daddy God couldn't fix if he fell on his knees and prayed."

"You know that's not him."

"I know that, and I've been knowing him a lot longer than you, but he still doing wrong by not sending you to law school."

"I'm going to go. It's just going to take more time. Next year I'll apply for loans and scholarships. I'll need to work, save my money."

"Yeah, what about you meeting some man and you get the hot pants for him? You gonna settle down and make a baby like anybody else. That's only natural. Way I see it, you gotta go to law school now, 'cause if you don't, you might never go."

"Pie, you don't have to worry, I promise," Trisha said, wrapping her arms around Pie's large waist.

Pie pulled away and started on the walls, but she abruptly stopped, dropping the sponges into the bucket and stormed from the kitchen, muttering. She returned with her purse.

"How much is that law school gonna cost you?"

"UCLA? About ten thousand."

"Okay, here," Pie said, and handed her a signed check with no amount written in.

"Now, come the fall, you use that for your first year."

Trisha glanced at the check and handed it back to Pie.

"Pie, you need your money. I'll do fine."

Pie shook her head, took the check, and closed Trisha's hand around it.

"I wouldn't be giving you the check if I couldn't afford it. I like money. That's why I saved it. I was always proud to work for the Bells. Your daddy made sure I got my money in the right accounts. I'm leaving all my money to you and that old man of mine who just sits there watching shows all day. You just getting some of the money sooner that you gonna get later, anyway."

Trisha gave Pie a hug and tried not to cry, but she couldn't help herself.

"I'm gonna go clean that little bathroom your daddy uses when he don't want nobody to know he's smoking a pipe."

Pie headed off, leaving Trisha the opportunity to pull herself together. She couldn't stop thinking about the check, using it for school. Pie's word was good.

She found Pie cleaning the already spotless mirror in the bathroom off the foyer that nobody used but her daddy.

"Pie, I just can't accept this money. Like I said, if I don't go this fall, I'll go the next."

"I don't want to hear all that," Pie said, turning away to scrub the tile in the bathtub.

"But, Pie . . ."

"It's that Jordan. You ready to tie that boy down, but you need to finish your education first."

"Jordan?"

"'Least Jordan got a use for girls. I know you talking to that David. When you gonna drop that boy? He's calling you all the time talking 'bout nothing."

"I didn't get the messages."

"I didn't take them down. He don't got nothing to say. What's going on with this Jordan?"

"He stopped seeing the other girl."

"See, now you cookin'."

"But I feel like I should talk to her. Find out exactly what's going on."

"Why don't you ask the boy?"

"He says it's over between them."

"Ain't that good enough for you?"

"No, I don't believe him. He's still in love but won't admit it. I'm going to invite her out for coffee and ask her if they're really broken up."

"What you really doing all this for?"

Trisha sighed and tried to avoid Pie's steely gaze, but Pie circled around until she could look Trisha right in the eye.

"I want to see for myself what has him so head over heels. If she sounds like a idiot, then I'll know he just likes pretty girls. There'll be no point in pretending we can have something serious."

"Well, if you do go out with this chickie, don't you take your eyes off her."

"Why?"

"Listen, I've been around. Sometimes these little chickies get crazy enough to do anything to keep their man. Even put some poison in your drink."

"I didn't think about that."

"Well, you better."

Pie, through with giving advice, went back to scrubbing the toilet.

Trisha returned to the kitchen and dialed. She let the

phone ring long enough to embarrass herself if someone picked it up. She heard a soft "Hello" on the other end.

"May I speak with Daphne?"

"This is she."

Trisha's heart raced.

"Daphne, this is Trisha Bell, Jordan's friend."

"Oh, hi. Jordan's spoken of you often."

"He has?" Trisha asked, without thinking.

"Yes, all compliments."

For a long moment Trisha couldn't mouth the words.

"Daphne, I know this is going to sound strange, but if you have some time, I really would like to have coffee with you."

149

"Coffee?"

"Yes, I thought we could talk."

Another long pause. This time on Daphne's end.

"Sure. How about this afternoon, Charlotte's on State? Threeish? Is that good for you?"

"Yes, it is."

"Good, I'll see you there."

Trisha hung up the phone feeling light-headed, as though she had been drinking. She was going to do it, meet her, see for herself what had so captivated Jordan.

After showering she did her nails and hair, and dressed faster than she had ever dressed. With only ten minutes to spare, she rushed outside and raced to the SUV. At the edge of the driveway, she saw her father's Saab laboring up the hill. Trisha's stomach sank. If they saw her, that would be it. She'd never make that appointment with Daphne. Trisha hit a quick right uphill to the San Marcos Pass to avoid having to greet her parents. She slid down in the seat, but through the rearview mirror she could see her father on the passenger's side for the first time in his life. His gaunt face looked tense, probably because her mother was driving his precious car.

It was very hard to find a place to park on State Street, and a woman had to be cautious. Seemingly most of the nuts, panhandlers, and skinheads hung out south of De La Guerra. Charlotte's, though, was a very nice café. She had been there once with David. Trisha wondered if Charlotte's was where Daphne and Jordan met for romantic rendezvous.

She entered the café and surveyed the tables, hoping she'd see Daphne before she was seen. Luckily, the room was almost empty, just a few couples, but no solo, well-dressed, beautiful exotic with a mess of unruly curls. That was a relief. Trisha wanted the high ground. Certainly, Daphne wouldn't have a problem spotting her, a single black bean on a bed of white rice.

After some twenty minutes Trisha noticed the headline of a discarded newspaper on the way to the rest room. The Harlem Globetrotters were suing the City of Santa Barbara for racism and police misconduct for arresting them in a jewelry store heist. Trisha shook her head. Santa Barbara deserved to pay through the nose. A half hour passed and she began to wonder if she was being stood up. Then, ready to leave, she saw a tall, attractive woman doing a serious sprint in heels across State. It had to be Daphne, all in white—stockings, shoes, some almost fairy-tale dress, puffing on a cigarette that she discarded halfway across the street. Trisha had chosen a seat that wasn't instantly visible from the door. She watched Daphne enter the restaurant, then she snatched up the newspaper and pretended to be engrossed. Just from the glimpse of her she could see how pretty she was, like a cross between Ingrid Bergman and Sonya Braga; an actress right out of those 1940s romances, distracted, pretty, and always in need of being rescued.

"Trisha?" Daphne asked, shyly. "Sorry I'm late. My mother needed me to run errands."

Trisha stood and they shook hands. Maybe she should have stayed seated; Daphne was almost a half foot taller than she was, but some of that was those heels.

"Thanks for meeting me. I know it's strange to have coffee with someone you don't know."

"Well, I can't say I'm not curious about you."

"You are?"

Daphne laughed.

"Let's be honest. We're both friends of Jordan. He's a good friend. I'm trying to understand him."

"In what way?"

"Oh, I don't know. How long have you known him?"

"A little more than a year."

A waiter walked by and Daphne gestured for his attention. They ordered drinks; for herself a latte and for Trisha an iced tea. Trisha would never bring that drink to her lips; Pie had ruined that with her poison warning. After the drinks were ordered, awkward glances exchanged, and a long painful pause, Daphne got to the point.

"Jordan means a lot to you?"

Trisha found herself almost unable to answer.

"I'm not sure I'm ready to admit that. I don't know if he's worth all the trouble."

"Trouble meaning, am I involved with Jordan?" Daphne asked.

"Yes, I guess that's the question I'd like answered."

"No, we're no longer seeing each other."

Trisha believed her. Somehow, she knew she was telling the truth.

"Did it just not work out?"

"No, it's complicated. But Jordan is special. I wouldn't do this for any other man. I knew you would be a good person and it would be okay to reassure you that Jordan and I are just friends."

152

"But why was it complicated? Was there a reason for you breaking up?"

Daphne smiled weakly.

"Actually, we were never a serious couple. We just dated. And . . . someone returned who's very important to me."

"An old boyfriend?"

"Yes, exactly."

"Well, that changes everything."

"It does."

"You must be very happy," Trisha said.

As if hitting a switch, Daphne's mood changed instantly. Her ease and poise disappeared; in its place was gloom.

"I'd better be going," she said, flatly.

"I should go too. I'm supposed to wait for a plumber to come finish installing a shower in our guest house. We're trying to rent it out, that and the main house," Trisha said.

"You are?"

"Actually, it's a little studio my mother likes to call a guest house."

"Where do you live?"

"On San Antonio Road, near the Pass."

"Oh, you'll have no problem renting that. It's very pretty and so close to the mountains."

Trisha nodded, but the truth was, many whites seemed uncomfortable renting from blacks, even in nice neighborhoods.

They walked out of the café together, both so distracted that neither paid. A waiter burst out of the door behind them waving the bill for two untouched drinks.

Trisha was parked a little farther up the street so they walked together, but not a word was exchanged. Trisha wanted to make another go at conversation, but she was too caught up in Daphne's dark mood.

"Is there something wrong? Are you feeling okay?" Trisha asked, when they reached the car.

Daphne tried to smile, but it was halfhearted.

"I just feel a little overwhelmed right now," Daphne said, as they parted.

Trisha watched David's muscular, dark body swim lap after lap in the pool. A really beautiful man, she thought, when he finally tired and pulled himself free of the pool and stretched out at her feet. She shifted the deck chair so she wouldn't be staring directly at his Speedo-covered ass.

"Girl, when are you going to try the water?"

Trisha shook her head. David stood up and began to massage her shoulders.

"Don't even think about throwing me in."

"I'm not. I just hope you'll fly up to San Francisco with

me. We'll stay at the Saint Francis, go to a few nice clubs. It'll be wonderful."

"But you still haven't explained . . ."

"Oh, not that again. You have to trust me. I'm not the only one. Many men choose . . . even though we have complex natures. We discover how we want to live and then we live it. Everything is possible."

David's agenda was broader than she knew what to do with, and his explanation, his story, the story he had been telling bits and pieces of for the last few weeks, made him even more bewildering.

"It's not about making love to a man. I don't have a problem with that, but I need more than that. With men it's always about the physical or money. I tried that life with an open mind, and it's not enough for me."

When David had first confessed all this to her, she wasn't allowing herself to believe it. What she wanted to say but couldn't bring herself to do was *Be for real!* Instead, she just tried to put a damper on his marriage fantasy, sighing and shaking her head whenever he mentioned it. Somehow she thought he'd get the message without her having to spell it out for him, but that didn't work. That head of his had to be made of mighty hard wood.

Now, as he sunned himself at her feet, looking as content as an old dog, she realized that her plot to make Jordan jealous had gotten out of hand. David seemed to think she would marry him even knowing he was gay.

"I want a family more than anything," he said.

"It won't work."

"I don't want to spend the rest of my life unfulfilled."

She shook her head.

"But you'll never want me for me. It'll be because you want something else. You want to be a father and a husband, but what about love? We're supposed to be joyful, but you'll be dutiful. I don't think that's enough."

David's face grew tense.

"Trisha, you have to trust me. I'm telling you the truth. If that isn't enough for you, I don't know what else to say. You must believe me."

"David, I'm the last one who should be saying this, but I don't think you can choose."

He knelt beside her and kissed her cheek.

155

"But I have. Sex isn't the issue. It's how I want to live my life," he said, while drying himself off with a taut towel, straining muscle to show off muscle.

"David, I do believe you. I want you to be happy, but what you're asking of me, I'm not capable of."

David ran his fingers along her arm.

"You know I love you."

Trisha pulled away angrily.

"You can't. You can't love me like a man loves a woman."

David laughed, surprising Trisha. She wanted him to leave.

"You'll find someone willing to do what you want."

"I want you, Trisha."

"That's because you can't have me."

"We'll see about that. You'll see how wrong you are."

"Go, David! Just leave!"

"Trisha?"

"Go!"

Enraged, Trisha kicked aside the deck chair as she stood.

"You just aren't listening to me," David said with a stricken look.

"No, you're the one who isn't listening! You told me your plans and I told you I'm not going to be part of them."

"Well, if you want to be a bitch about it."

Trisha's hand whipped up and slapped him hard.

"Get out!"

David hesitated, his hands clenched into fists. He grabbed her wrist and pulled her close.

"You're not listening to me!" he shouted.

She heard the sound of a screen sliding open and footsteps. There was her father striding towards them with golf club in hand.

"Hey, young man! What do you think you're doing?"

"Dad, stop!"

David raised his arms in protest, but Mr. Bell swung. David dived to avoid the blow.

"Who are you? Who do you work for?" Mr. Bell yelled, but David didn't answer because he was too busy swimming to the deep end of the pool. Even so Mr. Bell was on him, swinging the club inches above his head.

"What do you want? Why are you threatening my family?"

David again tried to pull himself from the pool, and again Mr. Bell blocked his way out with sizzling swings.

"Trisha, what's wrong with him! Help!"

"I don't know what's wrong with him, but I do know what's wrong with you. You're totally and completely stuck on yourself!" Trisha said, and gently led her father away from an astonished David.

CHAPTER 10

Somehow she thought if she just sat in the serenely empty, bare-walled, off-white room that was her studio apartment, that would be enough to exorcise this demon. If she gave it all away, everything, he wouldn't have anything to claim. She'd be as bare as the room, a container of nothing. What use could that be to him, a crop of misery for him to harvest?

How had she come to this, fighting for her life once again? She became what he wanted her to be; an uncomplaining, docile possession.

She was a figment of his imagination.

If she wanted a lawn to lull upon, cool grass between her toes, a breeze, trees growing along a stream, she'd have to free herself.

He wanted more from her, another figment.

She didn't need the pill, though he accused her of lying. She controlled that by running, running and sweating and working herself to exhaustion. Her fertility was gone because she didn't want to be pregnant for him. He strained against her to start a flood, but the river was dry.

His seed had entered her and it died.

Jordan's didn't.

Frank had always wanted a boy, but she knew she'd give birth to a girl.

She heard a light knock. It trailed off as though whoever it was was embarrassed to be knocking.

"It's open," she called. From around the opened door Jordan appeared, smiling awkwardly.

"Hey, how are you doing? I was driving by and I thought I'd check in."

She almost laughed at the silliness. Even though she wouldn't look at him, wouldn't turn her head from the white wall she had been looking at all morning, she could feel how uncomfortable he was with the image of what she was now. Pale, hair cut closer than his, thinner than he had ever seen her.

"Are you . . . getting over something? I . . ."

Daphne slowly shook her head.

"No, I'm fine. I just haven't been sleeping."

Jordan started toward her, but her eyes stopped him dead.

"You should go."

"Go, why? Am I intruding?"

"It has nothing to do with you."

Jordan's face hardened.

"It's this Frank? What's he doing to you?"

Daphne smiled faintly.

"This is me. This is all my choice. He has nothing to do with it."

"But you don't look . . ."

"He doesn't want me to look like this. He wants me to be beautiful."

Jordan shrugged, not knowing what to say.

"He's coming. You shouldn't be here."

"Listen, I'm not worried about him. It's you. What do your parents say?"

"They can't help me."

"Let me help you."

"You can't help me."

They both heard the sound of a car pulling up.

"It's him," Daphne said.

"It's okay," Jordan replied.

One sharp knock and Frank entered, more casual this time. Maybe as a concession to laid-back Santa Barbara, he wore crisp blue jeans and a black blazer.

"Greetings. I wondered when you'd come by and talk sense to Daphne."

Jordan didn't know what to make of this hipster with hardly enough hair left to make that ponytail he wore presentable.

"You know, Jordan, I think we need to talk."

"Talk?"

"Yes, but alone would be better."

Frank glanced at Daphne.

"Excuse us," he said.

Daphne quickly left the studio through the back door and went out onto the deck that overlooked the Riviera.

Surprised at how fast she had responded to Frank's suggestion, Jordan assumed the worst.

"What's up with that?"

"What's up with what?" Frank asked, sitting on the edge of the bed.

"There's room," he said, patting the mattress. "Daphne isn't much into furniture."

"You say something and she just jumps. She cleared out like she was frightened of you."

Frank laughed.

"Oh, you think I'm abusing her. No, I've never touched the girl with evil intent. She's just very responsive to suggestion."

"Oh, is that right?" Jordan said.

"Yes, but you need to know how to talk to a woman. You might not know how."

Jordan felt it roiling up, hot anger directed at this smug bastard. He rushed Frank, but as he tried to swing at Frank's bald head, he found himself falling hard, landing and blacking out for a moment.

"What is this? I mean, you really want to fight for this woman?"

Jordan lay wheezing, trying to catch his wind.

"You shouldn't lead with your jaw. That'll get you knocked on your ass every time."

Jordan grunted.

"Jordan, let me ask you, have you done time? You don't look the type. I'm not saying you're soft, but you seem like . . . how would I say it . . . soft."

Jordan finally managed to get his feet back under him. He

eyed Frank; he looked slow, but he had quick hands, and he hit pretty fucking hard. He tensed, getting ready to try it again.

Frank held out a finger.

He pulled up a pants leg and revealed the dull metal of a small gun.

"Before you decide to have another swing at me, I think you need to ask yourself what's going on here. Do you think I'm the one who made Daphne this way?"

Jordan rubbed the back of his head, glaring warily at Frank.

"I don't know, man. I don't know you but you act like some lowlife pimp!"

"Listen, I'm trying to help her."

"She was fine before you came to town."

"Yeah, blame it on me. I've been trying to hold her together for years."

"Then explain it, this influence you got going. You show up and she gets weird, stops talking to people, drops out of school."

"I think that's because she doesn't belong here. This isn't her world. Her world is my world," Frank said.

"What gives you the right to say that?"

"Well, for one thing she's my wife."

Jordan stood up quickly and again started toward him but stopped at a respectful distance.

"Why do you lie?"

Frank laughed.

"Do you need to hear it from her? Daphne!"

Daphne appeared as though she had been waiting by the door.

"Daphne, how long have we been married?"

"Five years," she said, without emotion.

Jordan shook his head and walked to the door.

"Listen, Jordan, don't leave without saying your good-byes. You're good for Daphne."

"I don't know what kind of game you're trying to run on me, but . . ."

He waved Jordan off.

"Ask Daphne. She'll explain it to you."

Frank adjusted his jacket and headed outside without a glance backward.

Jordan couldn't bring himself to look in Daphne's direction. He wanted to go, but somehow her silence held him there.

"Daphne, I'm getting out of here."

He started for the door but stopped, waiting for an answer. A reaction, anything. But she was distant, almost serene.

"So, is he lying?"

In a voice that sounded harsh from disuse, she responded.

"He's telling the truth."

"Why didn't you tell me?"

She shook her head.

"I don't know. I wanted to forget I married him."

"Why don't you divorce him?"

"I've tried."

"What do you mean you've tried? You can just do it."

"He won't let me."

"Daphne, he doesn't own you. You aren't his Sally Hemmings. You have your own mind."

"If I'm not with him . . . I have my own mind."

"What happens if you're with him?"

"I have his mind."

"I've known some women like you. They hand over their souls to guys and become property, but those women had to stand for beatings. You, you have something different going here. You've got all the money you need to tell Frank to go fuck himself. I don't get it, but I don't have to. It's your life."

Daphne smiled weakly and hung her head.

"I'll see you around."

She didn't look up as he closed the door.

Mr. Bell usually avoided answering the door, and with Pie staying with them to help with his convalescence, he had even less reason to respond to the doorbell. But something was up; no amount of psychotherapy could convince him otherwise. He clutched his golf club and threw the door open.

"Yes!" he said.

The white girl standing in the doorway made him instantly uncomfortable, even though he was the one gripping the golf club, ready to do damage with it. First of all, he wasn't sure she was white, and that threw him off. She looked like some of the Italian girls he had seen when he was in the service, but she didn't look healthy. Maybe it was the white sacklike dress she wore, calling to mind religious devotees, or the close-cropped hair, but more than anything it was the frightened expression on her face; the same fear he had managed to keep hidden—but now, after all these years, it had surfaced like a submarine through thin arctic ice.

"Did they send you?"

"Send me? I'm a friend of Trisha's."

"Are they after you?"

He sensed he had frightened her a bit because she inched away.

"Wait, don't go! Who's after me? You can tell me. I won't be angry."

Those words did nothing to calm her. She retreated farther down the driveway.

"Mr. Bell, why in heaven you answering the door with a golf club in your hand like you gonna hit somebody?" Pie asked, snatching the golf club from him.

"Hey, miss! Hey there!"

164

Pie's voice boomed down to the road, stopping Daphne cold. Pie lumbered down the driveway and escorted Daphne to the house.

"What you say your name is?" Pie asked, as they approached Mr. Bell.

"Daphne."

"Daphne, I'm Pie, and this is Mr. Bell, Trisha's daddy. Don't you mind that golf club. He carries that thing everywhere."

Mr. Bell eyed her.

"Maybe I should be going."

"Aw, no, sugar. You look hot and tired. Don't tell me you walked up that big hill?"

"Yes, but it wasn't so bad."

"Well, you coming in the house to cool off. Get you a nice lemonade or something."

"I think I should . . ."

Before Daphne could protest, Pie grabbed her firmly around the arm and led her into the coolness of the house. In-

side, Mr. Bell made a hard right and retreated to the den. Pie
guided a relieved Daphne to the master bedroom where Lady
Bell was packing boxes for the move.

"Mrs. Bell, look here, one of Trisha's friends."

Lady Bell, in a pretty, bright pink sundress with her gray
hair in a matching ribbon, looked up smiling. Delighted at the
interruption, she crossed the room and surprised Daphne with
a hug.

"Trisha should be right back. She's out finding more boxes
for our move."

"I really don't mean to impose."

"You're not imposing in the least. Let me get you some
lemonade."

Daphne shrugged and followed the two women to the
kitchen.

The backseat full of boxes, Trisha couldn't see anything out of
the rearview mirror. Everything annoyed her; the beautiful day,
cool and windy, white clouds capping the mountains, the stupid move, and especially the fact that Jordan hadn't arrived like
he said he would to help out with the heavy lifting. Dad was
supposedly doing fine but she had serious doubts about the
doctor's judgment. Last week she saw him slip into the bathroom, shut the door, and have a shouting match with himself.
Trisha was so stressed that some nights she woke herself with
the sound of her own teeth grinding.

At the house she struggled to get boxes out of the SUV,
then arrange them into a balanced stack, higher than her eyes.
She managed to walk to the door without tripping or dropping
anything, but her fingers fumbled around endlessly trying to

find the chime. Finally, she did, and she waited for help, but none came. Disgusted, she dropped the boxes and unlocked the door. She called out but no one answered. More disgusted that they had cut out, she started back to the car for more boxes, then she heard their voices out by the pool, and another voice that was only vaguely familiar.

"Your friend is here. You sure she can be trusted?"

Startled at the unexpected sound of her father's voice, she turned to see him with the damn golf club.

"What friend? You mean Jordan?"

"I mean the white young lady with the short hair."

"I don't know any young white ladies with short hair."

"Maybe she isn't white. What do you call it, Creole?"

"I don't know anybody who fits that description. Are you sure it's not Mama's friend?"

Mr. Bell's face fell slack.

"They've finally broken in," he said, running faster than she could remember him doing.

He flung open the screen door and ran through the backyard to the pool where Pie and her mother were having drinks with a young, short-haired white woman.

Daphne!

Trisha sprinted by Mr. Bell and stopped directly in front of Daphne, who seemed to be having a fine time with Lady Bell and Pie. Daphne looked much different, almost bald, thinner—too thin, like she hadn't eaten in days, and sickly pale as though she had been shunning sunlight since Trisha had seen her last.

"What's going on here!" she said, directly to Daphne.

Lady Bell was surprised at her daughter's tone.

166

"Daphne's been telling us of her travels. She's on her way to India."

"India?" Trisha repeated with relief, but it was short-lived because Mr. Bell approached with golf club at the ready.

"She's working for them. She's the one who's been listening! She's the one who's been listening to me," Mr. Bell shouted.

"Ain't nobody listening to you," Pie said, gruffly.

He immediately calmed down; paranoid or not, Pie wasn't going to humor him.

"Dad, I know her. She's a friend from school. She took a class with Jordan."

167

"Well, I had to drop."

"Oh," Trisha said, looking more pleased than she wanted to.

Deflated, Mr. Bell retreated into the house after a mumbled "Excuse me."

"We're not moving," Lady Bell said to Trisha.

"What? How?"

"I haven't cleared it with your father yet, but Daphne wants to rent the guest house."

"The guest house?"

Trisha shook with confusion—go out for boxes and come home to a nightmare.

"It's only for a few months. Time to get things in order for the trip," Daphne said.

"But it's a great idea. We'll keep it rented and your father won't have any reason to move."

"Yeah, but your mama actually got to find someone who ain't gonna sweet-talk her out of the rent," Pie said.

Lady Bell held up a check for two thousand dollars.

"Excuse us," Trisha said, gesturing for Daphne to follow her. "We're going for a walk."

Trisha led Daphne to the other end of the deck, but even at that distance she could feel their eyes, so she continued leading Daphne on in the direction of the park. She wanted to shout the question, "Why have you decided to ruin my life!" But instead she walked at an increasing pace with Daphne seemingly content to be led. After a hot and dusty walk by more modest homes on the downhill slope, they reached Stowe Grove Park and the cool shade of oak trees. Trisha found a reasonably clean picnic table where they sat across from each other, but neither looked the other in the eye. Whatever was going on with Daphne, it couldn't justify this intrusion into her life.

"I know you're shocked to see me. I didn't mean for this to happen. Mrs. Pie and Lady Bell are so sweet, one thing just led to another."

"It's just Pie. Everybody calls her that. I have since I was a baby. Renting the guest house, that's out of the question."

"Yes, it's a little much to even consider."

"But why would you? You just met me, and that was just because I was jealous of your relationship with Jordan."

Daphne looked Trisha right in the eye. Trisha could feel it coming, the reason why, and it made her queasy. It would be a damn good reason.

"I'm trying to hide from my husband."

Trisha felt her jaw drop open and hang there.

"You're married?" she finally managed to say.

"Yes. I've been married for the last five years, since I turned eighteen."

Nervously, Trisha scratched her arms.

"Does Jordan know?"

"He knows now."

Trisha turned away to collect her thoughts.

"This husband, is he hurting you?"

"He doesn't hurt me, he controls me."

"Honestly, Daphne, I don't see how I can be of help to you. You can divorce him. Get a restraining order . . ."

"I know. I haven't lived with him for years, but I can't break away. He pulls me back in. I can never go too far."

Trisha stood there, in a shade of an oak, feeling flushed, embarrassed to know all of this about Daphne.

169

"Ever since we had coffee I've thought about you. I thought about what Jordan told me about you, and I admire how you don't compromise. I thought maybe you could help me."

"Help you? You're the one who just paid two thousand dollars to live in a studio that we couldn't rent out for the last two years. It's barely enough for a bed."

"That's all I'll need. A little space to disappear into for a couple of months away from my family and Frank."

"But what about Jordan?"

"Jordan . . ."

"He's still crazy about you."

"I don't think so. Not after finding out about Frank."

Trisha sighed and reached for the distraction of a leaf.

"You won't know I'm here," Daphne said, almost in a whisper.

"But why here? What about a motel? Maybe some place in Goleta?"

"You probably think I'm insane. This isn't your problem, but Frank controls people. My family can't handle him, neither can my friends. Your family is outside the circle of his influence. I never thought about it before, but you and your family live in your own world. White people live in theirs. Frank wouldn't find me here."

It all came together for Trisha.

"I don't know what to think."

Daphne shook Trisha's hand.

"I won't cause you any problems."

She waved to Trisha and took off walking at a very fast pace. For someone who looked so fragile, she was in great shape, Trisha thought, as she puffed up the hill to her house.

CHAPTER 11

Weeks passed and not a glimpse of Daphne. Trisha began to wonder if Daphne actually was in there, in a bleak, almost windowless box of a guest house that Trisha imagined only a hard-up grad student would consider renting. She assumed it had started out as a cabana, but the previous owners ran out of money and thought they could get away with something halfway between a utility shack and a Santa Barbara studio; and a Santa Barbara studio is anything with three walls and a bucket. She remembered her father joking about it being their own slave quarters. Lady Bell was uncomfortable with the newfound windfall, and even more so because Daphne was never around to invite to dinner. Mr. Bell had Lady Bell deposit the check as soon as possible to ensure that it would clear, but Trisha had no doubt.

"Do you ever see her go in there?" Trisha asked Mr. Bell, but even with his paranoid need to know, he didn't have much to add.

"Sometimes I hear the pool gate opening," he said gravely.

Out of sight but not out of mind. Trisha was relieved that Daphne had conveniently vanished before graduation. Graduation would be her salvation, she hoped. She'd be on her way to starting a new life away from family, and now, this weird situation with Daphne. She prayed that it would come off without trouble, even if Daphne seemed more a hapless ghost than a femme fatale.

Graduation day arrived. Lady Bell had been ready since early morning for the afternoon ceremony. Pie arrived with a cake big enough to feed two wedding parties and just in case they were needed, some of her sweet potato pies. Pie seemed to produce them like magic, but the truth was, Pie had a huge freezer in her garage, and sweet potato pies freeze very well.

Pie glared at Trisha.

"Where's your cap and gown?" Pie asked.

"I'll put it on there."

"You put that thing on now."

"Pie!"

"Child, I want to see how that thing fits on you."

Reluctantly, Trisha put on the gown. It fit poorly but she didn't care. She would just return it when the ceremony was over, but Pie led her into the kitchen where she had her sewing kit.

"This ain't gonna take but a minute. Why you so impatient? You done waited all these years to graduate, you can wait 'til I finish you up."

Trisha could only nod her agreement as Pie ripped a seam and started work. As usual, Pie's logic won out.

As Jordan was readying for Trisha's graduation, he noticed a black BMW with a license plate "Carpe Diem!" turn into the driveway. A car door slammed, and he saw a man walking to the front door. The entrance no one used except for strangers. Frank! Panicked, Jordan rushed for the back-door as Frank knocked on the front. Through the back-door window he saw that Frank had blocked the Triumph in.

173

No longer burning mad, ready to rush Frank even if meant getting slammed, he beat a retreat. Daphne had burned him, and he wasn't about to lift a finger for her.

Outside, he ducked behind the Triumph, then went on across to the safety of a strip mall congested with people. Then he thought about it, having to flee from his own house. This wasn't about Daphne, this was about him. He couldn't do it. He returned to the driveway ready for whatever. Frank had returned to the BMW, waiting for Jordan like he expected to collect serious debt. Jordan hesitantly approached the driver's side, trying to stay clear of the side mirror.

"Hey, you looking for me?"

Frank exploded from the BMW so fast he almost caught Jordan with the swinging car door.

"Where is she?" he demanded, all the cool demeanor from their first encounter gone, now just a red-faced rage.

"What are you talking about?" Jordan replied, stepping back to create some space between them.

"Is she in there?" Frank demanded, pointing to the house.

"Daphne? Be for real! She's a married woman. I don't fuck around with married women."

"You're involved in this!"

"I don't have a damn thing to do with this. She's your problem, not mine."

Frank lunged for Jordan, but Jordan twisted away and threw a punch to his ribs. Frank let out a *whoosh* and slumped against the car. Jordan backpedaled away and waited for the next move.

174

"Pretty brave. You still want to mix it up."

"No, I don't, but you're not beating me down this time."

"Listen, I know you're in on this. I'm trying to be polite. I could just kick the back door of this dump in and see for myself, or you could unlock the door."

"You got no reason. I'm telling you the truth."

Frank laughed.

"Okay. Well, I'll see for myself."

Frank headed for the door, and at the top of the rickety steps, he leaned back to get off a good kick.

"Wait, it's open," Jordan said at the last moment.

Frank sneered at him and flung the door open.

Jordan wondered how long he was going to be in this fucked-up situation. Then he heard the sound of Art's busted muffler and of course, he parked behind the BMW.

"Hey, J, whose beauty is this?" Art asked.

"Daphne's husband. You don't want to go in the house."

"Man, I got to take a dump! I don't give a fuck if Godzilla is in there."

Art rushed in. A few moments later as Jordan expected, Art came back walking so fast he looked to be skipping.

"Who's that big fucking narc? You didn't buy something off his ass?"

Jordan shook his head.

"So, what's he doing?"

"He's looking for his wife."

"Oh."

Art looked seriously panicked.

"His wife?"

"Yeah, it's Daphne."

Art glanced back at the house, then started inching to his VW Bug.

"What is this? Is he on some revenge trip?"

"I don't know, but he does keep a gun."

Art hopped in the Bug, cranked and gunned the engine, and began backing out.

"Let's get out of here and call the fucking police."

Jordan turned to Art and didn't see a grim-faced Frank burst from the house.

"Move your car," Frank said to Art, as if he weren't in the process of pulling out. As he started his own car, he called to Jordan.

"I hope you're not lying to me. I'll be back. I'm not fucking around this time."

Jordan arrived for the graduation almost on time. He should have been early, but he couldn't get himself off the couch, sitting there plotting strategies with Art about how to handle maniac white men.

"You need to tell this idiot to stay away."

"I did, but I'm not prepared to shoot him, so I guess I can't stop him from looking for his wife."

Jordan could tell from Art's smirk that he didn't believe him when he said he didn't know Daphne had a husband. He couldn't blame him.

The graduation ceremony was held by the lagoon under blue skies and on newly planted sod. The graduates milled around in their black robes, waiting to receive their marching orders. Campus dignitaries paraded to the portable stage big enough to handle the assembly line procession of students. Jordan found Trisha and her family where Trisha said they'd be, in front of the faculty club. Mr. Bell wore a drab gray suit, Lady Bell wore an aquamarine suit that blended perfectly with the green-grass foreground and the blue ocean behind it. Pie had on a fur with a horrific little fox head around her shoulders and a pillbox hat. She was more excited than Trisha's parents. Trisha looked stylish in her Pie-hemmed robe while everyone else seemed buried in the bulky black severity of the graduation robes. She smiled when she saw Jordan walking toward her. He kissed her briefly, and took pains to shake Mr. Bell's hand firmly and to kiss Pie and Lady Bell.

"You're only twenty minutes late," Trisha whispered to him.

"Really?" he said, and kissed her again.

Trisha left them to join the graduates as they began the procession. Trisha sat proudly among her AKA sorors, twenty or so young black women with the highest grade-point average of any of the Greek organizations on campus.

Lady Bell could no longer suppress her joy to see her last child finish college, even if her husband's presence hindered her from showing the full extent of her happiness.

"Lady," Mr. Bell said, trying to calm her enthusiasm, but she ignored him.

The ceremony went surprisingly quickly. It was the black graduates' turn to walk the stage, divided into frats or sororities or friends or classmates; they received their diplomas together. Michelle, Trisha's closest friend and soror, raised her hands to the sky and shouted, "Thank you, Lord!" Then it was Trisha's turn. She walked quickly to the chancellor to the sound of sorors shouting, "Skee Wee!" Lady Bell popped up from her seat and applauded wildly. Even Mr. Bell stood and clapped. Pie, swaying like she was in church, clutched a handkerchief to her eyes.

Jordan was glad he had come.

Later that evening, at the graduation party for Trisha at the Bells', Pie brought out large trays of barbecued chicken wings for the buffet table by the pool. The house was starting to fill up with guests, and Jordan felt right at home and proud to find himself helping to host the party. Trisha was busy greeting everyone and accepting envelopes; Jordan hoped they were filled with money. She didn't have time for him, so he ended up in the kitchen watching Pie hastily prepare more refreshments.

"Boy, you must not be getting enough to eat." She stopped working long enough to fix him a plate.

"Pie, I'm okay, really."

"Aw, you know you want me to fix this up for you."

Jordan didn't disagree.

"So, you saw that friend of yours?"

"Friend? I don't have any friends here."

Pie cut her eyes.

"I mean outside of you guys," Jordan said.

"What about that girlfriend of Trisha's livin' in the back house?"

Jordan shrugged.

"You better ask that Trisha. We don't see the girl much, just a ghost opening doors every now and then leaving a light on, but that's it."

Jordon shrugged.

"So, you serious about my girl?"

"Trisha is great."

"You better be a man and go on and ask her; don't you be keeping her around like she's some piece of meat drying in a meat locker."

"Drying in a locker?"

"Y'all need to start planning. Getting married ain't no walk in the park."

"Getting married?" Jordan almost dropped his plate of chicken wings.

"That's what we talkin' about."

"That's what we're talking about?"

Pie scowled mightily at him.

"Do I look like I'm kidding?" she said.

"No."

"Ya got to take care of business."

Jordan lost his appetite for chicken wings. He put down the plate and then backed away. Pie closed in on him, picking the plate up.

"You ain't done with these. Don't be wasting food."

He quickly picked up the plate of wings, trying to inch away.

"No, you ain't gettin' off easy," Pie said, her hand clamping down on his wrist. "I'm not through with you."

Trapped and desperate, he thought of *White Fang*. He imagined showing up at the emergency room with a gnawed, bloody stump for a hand, and having to explain to a doctor that it was worth it.

"Hey, Jordan, I've been looking all over for you."

Saved by Trisha Bell!

"Pie, are you scaring Jordan? It looks like you got him cornered."

Jordan flashed a look of desperation to Trisha but she didn't seem to notice.

"I was tellin' him you two need to get married," Pie said, still clutching his wrist.

"Pie, don't tease him. He doesn't know how you tease."

"I ain't teasing, girl. I want him to know I'm dead serious."

Finally, Pie let go of the death grip she had on his wrist. Trisha didn't seem to be surprised or alarmed by Pie's statement. Jordan smiled awkwardly as he rubbed at his wrist, trying to get some feeling back into it.

"Well, you talk sense to that boy. He don't have time to waste. You two need to start on a family, not playing games chasing after each other."

Pie turned and headed back to the kitchen, and Jordan was very happy to see her go.

Trisha had changed into a short, sleeveless black dress, and she looked comfortable and happy.

"Don't let her worry you. I don't plan to force you to marry me yet."

"Thanks," Jordan said.

"I'll give you a few months to get your nerve up to ask."

He smiled as though she was joking—or at least he wanted to believe she was.

"So, what was Pie talking about? You have a girlfriend staying here?"

Trisha's mouth fell open.

"What?"

"Yeah, she said a girl we're both friends with is staying here."

Trisha looked away from him nervously.

"I've got to circulate."

He nodded, and Trisha hurried away without looking back.

Jordan knew. Daphne was staying there, and the thought confused and angered him. He couldn't get far enough away from the humiliation she had put him through. It was still an open wound for him, but now it seemed Trisha wanted to keep it fresh.

Was she there at the party?

A quick walk around to the pool, where most of the guests had gathered, didn't turn up any skinny, pale, short-haired girls who could pass for white. Not only was he confused at the idea of her being there, but what reason would there be for her to stay with the Bells?

Then he thought of Frank; that was more than reason enough. She must be trying to lose herself right under his nose. Maybe she hoped she'd find safe harbor with the

Bells. Jordan was so lost in thought, he didn't notice Trisha next to him.

"So you figured it out."

"Yeah," he said flatly.

"She needed help."

"This Frank, her husband, is dangerous. If he finds out, he'll come and get her," Jordan said.

"What do you think we should do?"

"You gotta ask her to leave."

Trisha frowned and looked away at the guests enjoying themselves; chatting, eating in the bright, harsh sun.

"I can't. You should have seen her; confused, frightened."

"How is she now?"

"She comes and goes; we hardly see her."

"Maybe I should talk to her," Jordan said.

"So you can be the knight in shining armor?"

"It's not about that."

"No, this is serious, Jordan. She wanted me to help her, not you. She could have asked you. She's here. I'm going to do everything I can for her."

"You're as crazy as she is."

Jordan felt Trisha's eyes on him as he walked out of the party and out of the house and got into his car.

Almost ten; the house was quiet. Everything was just about returned to its former order, thanks to Pie's desire to clean up the mess now, no matter how big a mess or how late. Trisha told her parents she was going to another graduation party, but instead she found herself in a lawn chair pulled close to the house in a gap of darkness between the glare of the pool lights. The timer went off at ten and then she was in complete darkness. The early summer evening was balmy, too comfortable. She started to drift, hearing fragments of disembodied conversation coming from the house; Pie's heavy voice, her mother's light one, the news shows her father listened to in the den. Then she heard light footsteps; then, illuminated by moonlight, Daphne. Trisha waited until she unlocked the door of the guest house before calling out to her in a whisper.

"Daphne! It's me, Trisha."

At first Daphne lingered half in the doorway as if she were deciding whether or not to shut the door. Trisha, sensing her indecision, hurriedly crossed the distance.

182

"Can we talk for a moment?" Trisha asked.

Daphne looked confused, but after a moment allowed Trisha into the guest house. Trisha waited patiently for Daphne to turn on the lights. Finally, after a long awkward moment, Trisha couldn't stand to be in the darkness any longer.

"Where are the lights?"

"Oh, the lights," Daphne said, and reached about the wall, fumbling as though she had never turned them on.

The lights revealed an empty room, spartan as a prison cell. There was a simple mat and a sheet covering it. A towel hung from a doorknob. The only indication that a person did more than sleep there was a few paperbacks resting next to a coffee cup and an open notebook.

"How are you doing?" Trisha finally asked.

"I'm okay. I was planning to write a few letters."

"Really?"

Daphne looked very sunburned and gaunt. She looked to Trisha like the homeless women on State Street.

"Congratulations. Someone slid an invitation under the door but I thought it would be awkward for me to come."

"I'm sure that was my mother. You should have come," Trisha said, lying through her teeth.

"No, I have imposed on you enough as it is."

"Imposed on us? We never hear you or see you. Pie says you're a ghost."

Daphne smiled for the first time. The gauntness, the tension in her face, lessened.

"Your mother tried to give half the rent back but I wouldn't take it."

Trisha shook her head, wondering if her mother wouldn't give away her last dollar.

"I'm been meaning to tell you, I'm leaving for India, tomorrow."

"Tomorrow?" Trisha repeated, feeling giddy and a little ashamed of it.

"When are you leaving?"

"In the morning."

"Let me give you a ride to wherever you're going. I know you've been doing all of this walking. You must be tired going up and down the hills."

"I hike from sunup until after dark. It's cleansing and meditative." Daphne paused and looked down at the ground. "A ride to my family home in Hope Ranch would be great."

"Sure, that's not a problem," Trisha said, and left the guest house in a hurry. She walked to the other side of the pool and sat heavily into the deck chair, wondering if Jordan had noticed that Daphne wasn't all there. No, she was too pretty and she wasn't as gone in the head back then. So much had

183

changed from the first time she saw Daphne. Then she was beautiful, composed, well dressed, and even though she hated to admit it, charming. Now, she looked like another burned-out hippie walking up the road toward the foothills. But Daphne wasn't searching for somewhere to crash. No, she was searching for visions and mortifying the flesh.

Trisha rose early, just after sunup, and hurried to the guest house, hoping Daphne would be ready to leave. She took a deep breath, calmed herself, and knocked sharply. No response. Again she knocked, but with the same result. Trisha was about to give up when she caught a glimpse of someone hiking through thick brush.

At the edge of their property on the hillside, it was very tough going, and it took a while for her to reach the railing and scramble over it.

"Good morning," Trisha said to Daphne.

Trisha glanced at Daphne's legs and saw blood trickling from several good scratches.

"I got caught a few times," Daphne said, holding up her sleeves and revealing long red welts. "My ankles are worse."

"Would you like breakfast before you go? Pie's a great cook."

Trisha was sure Daphne would have no interest in eating, but she nodded yes.

"I'll tell Pie you're coming. She has breakfast ready at seven-thirty or so."

Trisha watched Daphne disappear into the guest house; she seemed more out of it than yesterday. What did she plan to find in India except poverty and suffering? If she needed spirituality, she could find that anywhere. She didn't need to go around the world.

Unless she was running for her life.

At the breakfast table Mr. Bell drank his tea while reading an excruciatingly well-folded paper. Lady Bell busied herself sorting through a box of Bible-verse cards. Only Pie looked ready to boil over as the clock reached 8:10 A.M.

"So, where is this Daffy? I gotta serve breakfast; eggs are cooling, and the bacon's cold."

"I'll see," Trisha said.

Trisha walked outside wanting to scream at the top of her lungs; keeping her father waiting for breakfast was not a good idea. At Daphne's door again, Trisha knocked and waited but no response. She had probably already floated away to her new life as a crazy woman in India, Trisha thought, as she returned to breakfast.

Pie was stewing at the sink, glowering at her own reflection in the chrome of the faucet.

"You can serve breakfast. I'm not sure of what happened to Daphne," Trisha said, and sat down at the table just as the doorbell rang. She stood up to answer but Pie had already started for it. After a long moment she returned with Daphne.

"Good morning," Daphne said, sheepishly.

Trisha noticed the backpack in Daphne's hand. Probably halfway down the hill before she decided to return to have breakfast.

Daphne sat down quickly and stared at an empty plate.

"You picked a beautiful day for a trip. Do you travel much?" Lady Bell asked.

"I've been traveling for the last five years. This is my first trip home in a while."

"Where you off to now?" Pie asked, as she served breakfast. She gave Daphne a double serving of bacon and hash browns.

"India."

"What's in India? You know somebody there? That's where they got all them cows running around with them starving people, down on their knees worshipping them," Pie said.

For a long moment nothing was said. Mr. Bell looked up from his paper. Trisha couldn't see Daphne's eyes; she hoped she wouldn't bolt from the table and go screaming out the door.

"India is a very spiritual country."

"Child, if you looking for spiritual, just open your eyes and look," Pie said.

Daphne didn't say anything.

"Sometimes people search for what's right there in their face," Pie said.

Trisha realized she had thought the same thing that Pie had said, almost exactly. She didn't know what that meant, but it embarrassed her.

Daphne nodded, considering Pie's comment. She hadn't touched the bacon on her plate, but she had eaten almost all of the potatoes. Daphne chewed so thoroughly it was as though food wasn't something she was familiar with.

After breakfast Trisha and Daphne headed to the car for the drive to Hope Ranch.

"I hope Pie didn't make you too nervous. She's got strong opinions about everything."

"No, I like it when people tell me what they really think."

As Trisha unlocked the door for Daphne, she heard someone coming from the house.

"Y'all wait for me." It was Pie wiping her hands on the
apron as she pulled it from her waist.

Shrugging, Trisha looked at Daphne. Daphne smiled and
returned the shrug. Daphne offered the front seat to Pie but
she wouldn't go for it.

"Y'all just go about your business."

Trisha felt relieved that Pie had decided to accompany
them, even though dropping Daphne off now would be a
complicated adventure. Daphne slyly cast glances back at Pie
as if she expected a cuff on the back of the head, or maybe she
wanted a clue of what to expect next.

187

Trisha drove the poorly marked Hope Ranch Road, waiting for Daphne to give a signal to slow down, but Daphne
slipped back into herself, withdrawing even more the closer
they got to the house.

"Daphne, shouldn't it be right around here?"

Daphne looked up from gazing at her hands.

"Sorry, we passed it a half mile ago."

Trisha wanted to shake her awake but she contained it,
knowing she'd be out of her life in a few minutes. Finally, she
found space enough to turn around.

"Where to?" Trisha asked in a more demanding tone.

"It's the next driveway."

Driving up the winding brick-lined driveway, Trisha
thought of how much money Daphne's family must have; her
family home was a estate.

"Ya'll got a nice house here," Pie said, pulling herself up
on the back of Trisha's seat for a better view.

Well, this was it. Trisha thought, as she put the car in park, letting the engine idle. Daphne slid from the car and looked back at Trisha and Pie.

"You should come in and meet my parents," Daphne said with a little desperation in her voice.

"We really should be getting back . . ." Trisha replied, but Daphne continued to implore with her eyes.

"Aw, come on. The girl just want us to step in for a hot minute."

"But I don't want to impose."

"Trisha! Get out of the car. The girl invited us in."

Trisha cut the engine and slumped back as Daphne helped Pie from the backseat.

"Come on, girl. Don't be impolite," Pie said.

"Please, just for a minute," Daphne said, for a moment resembling that beautiful woman that Trisha had met not that long ago.

Resigned, Trisha opened the car door and followed Daphne and Pie across the broad lawn to the house.

Daphne unlocked the door and led them into the jungle-motif living room.

"Y'all got some interesting taste," Pie said, standing next to the dragon-fan sculpture. Trisha sat on the couch and looked around the vibrant green, art-filled room, wondering what the parents would be like.

Daphne returned with a thin, blond woman who looked too young to be Daphne's mother until she came close enough to reveal the gray at her temples and crow's feet at her eyes. She held on to Daphne like she might run away at any moment.

"Mrs. Pie, this is my mother, Denise Daniels."

"Pleased to meet you. You got a beautiful house and an interesting living room," Pie said, frowning.

"And this is Trisha Bell. She's a friend from school. I've been staying with them."

Mrs. Daniels looked at them with teary eyes.

"Thank you for opening your home to my daughter."

"Well, the child did pay rent so it wasn't all of that," Pie said.

Trisha instantly liked her, but red-eyed and puffy-faced, she looked to be at the end of her rope.

"Coffee?" she asked them.

Trisha again tried to decline.

189

"I really wouldn't want to impose."

Pie scowled.

"Don't pay no attention to this one. She don't say what she means."

Daphne glanced at Trisha.

"Please stay," she whispered.

"Sure, I'd like to stay for coffee if it's not too much trouble."

"Good," Mrs. Daniels said, and led them through the house to the veranda. After Trisha and Pie were seated, Mrs. Daniels and Daphne retreated to the kitchen, chattering like it was just another lunch with guests. Alone with Pie, Trisha wondered why Pie had insisted on coming and staying for coffee.

"What's with all this love you have for Daphne now? You thought she was a kook before."

Pie shook her head.

"She needs help. You don't invite trouble in, but once it's looking you in the face, you got to deal with it."

"Trouble?"

"All you got to do is look at her. You can see it."

"See what?"

"She's gonna have a baby," Pie whispered harshly.

Trisha screamed.

"Girl, calm yourself down!"

"I don't understand . . . what are you saying?"

"You know what it means. I said she's knocked up."

Trisha screamed again but this time Pie's hand shot across the table and flattened against her mouth.

"Girl, stop acting like you possessed!" Pie said.

Trisha tried to think of a coherent response, but the possibility of Daphne carrying Jordan's baby left her speechless.

Daphne returned with a tray of pastries and returned to the kitchen.

Pie gripped Trisha's hand and squeezed hard enough to distract her from glaring at Daphne.

"I don't know what to do about this. What am I supposed to even think?"

"You're not supposed to think nothing. You're a Christian. This ain't your mess. You just trying to do right."

Trisha sighed. What she wanted to do was brain Daphne with that heavy serving tray. Pie could be the Christian soldier, but she wanted to be the devil.

Mrs. Daniels brought in a tray of delicate cups and a silver coffeepot, and Daphne carried a bowl of sugar with both hands as though she might drop it. She stumbled almost immediately, bumping her mother.

Trisha knew why Mrs. Daniels looked frayed, with a daughter like Daphne.

"I don't want you to think I fret every time I don't hear

from Daphne, but these last few months I just didn't know what to think."

"You really don't have to worry about me," Daphne said.

"I couldn't help it. I thought you had decided to . . ."

"I know, go off for another year without a word. I told you I swore I'd never do that to you again," Daphne said, with conviction. "I've decided to return to India," she continued.

"Really?" Mrs. Daniels replied, barely showing her disapproval.

"The last time you were there, it wasn't very pleasant," she said.

"Then I didn't know what I was looking for, but this time . . . this time I'll stay and get my breath back. I'll be free of Frank. He hates India. He wouldn't set foot in the country."

"Yes, but that seems too much," Mrs. Daniels said.

"Yeah, and what kind of place is that to raise a baby?" Pie asked.

"What?" Mrs. Daniels said.

"A baby. Don't you know your girl is pregnant?" Pie asked.

Daphne sat there stone faced, but didn't deny it, as Mrs. Daniels, turning pale, looked as though she was going to faint.

Then the phone rang.

Mrs. Daniels rose from the table as if she were going to answer it, but instead collapsed back down.

"I'll get it," Daphne said, and rushed away. Mrs. Daniels' eyes followed her out of the room.

Pie shook her head. "You've been through the wringer with that one."

"Well, we never had to deal with this. This is a first."

191

"Mrs. Daniels, Pie is just guessing. She says she knows, but . . ." Trisha said.

"If it is true, I don't want to tell her father. That's the last thing he needs to hear."

Mrs. Daniels looked into Trisha's eyes as though she really knew Daphne.

"This is the first time I've seen her in more than a month, and now to learn this! My first grandchild and she wants to raise it twelve thousand miles away in India."

"We should go," Trisha said, standing up.

"Actually, I'm overwhelmed," Mrs. Daniels said, weakly.

192

"You look like you need someone to talk to," Pie said, and gestured for Trisha to come closer.

"Trisha, you go call your mother, Lady Bell. It's a blessing from God the way she can make people feel better."

"Call my mother?"

"Yeah, get her over here, now."

Trisha reached for the phone thinking she should be the one running off to India. She could imagine her mother matching Mrs. Daniels' grief ounce for ounce; two strangers falling into a river of tears. Trisha dialed and soon heard her mother's cheery voice.

She couldn't bring herself to relay Pie's message, so she handed the phone over, and Pie grumbled about the gravity of the situation and the need for her to get over there quickly.

After tiring of looking at Mrs. Daniels stretched out on the couch, pillow over her head, Trisha decided to wait outside for Lady Bell. There, leaning against a Greek revival column, she saw a black BMW sliding and trashing to the house, hurling gravel far enough that she flinched. The driver hit the horn sharply and a moment later Daphne appeared, hesitated for a moment on the porch, turning back to the house. A man shouted from the car, and she approached the BMW as though she was hypnotized. Trisha watched Daphne get in and felt her stomach sink. The car pulled away in another hail of gravel. Trisha returned to Pie, and Mrs. Daniels and told them of what she saw.

Mrs. Daniels sighed, then stood up and walked to the living room and collapsed again onto the couch, pulled a brocade pillow over her head, and wailed like a lost child.

193

CHAPTER 12

L ate morning limped into early afternoon, late afternoon crawled into early evening, but still Trisha sat planted in the
living room where the day had started, except for a too-
short walk to the pool where she had briefly sat in an
elaborately designed lawn chair underneath a bougainvil-
lea-covered trellis. Mostly, though, she stayed in the
hated jungle living room where she fantasized she was in
some disgusting *Tarzan* movie where she and Pie and her
mother were all noble savages helping Tarzan and Jane
work out their marital problems. Just as she predicted,
Lady Bell had the effect of causing Mrs. Daniels to burst
into tears with alarming frequency. Lady Bell cried right
along because she truly cared for this woman and shared
her anguish, though she had met the woman only six
hours ago. Trisha had her own private anguish. One

thing about being a virgin is you don't end up pregnant. Did Jordan even ask Daphne if she was using something? Probably not. He just humped, blindly humped away, grateful to be getting some. As a result he could be the father of a married woman's baby, a not one hundred percent sane married woman at that.

Then the thin-lipped, grim-faced Mr. Daniels arrived. Pie had terse words of consolation for him.

"God gave us children to torment us," she said before introducing herself, Trisha, and Lady Bell.

After hearing about the situation from Mrs. Daniels, he headed to the bar, offering everyone a drink and pouring himself a tumbler of gin. He then walked out.

But what was the point of all this? Trisha asked herself. Daphne left with that husband of hers; she was rational enough. She could be married to whomever she chose. Daphne and the monster were married; even monsters had the right to spend time with their spouses.

"I've done my best to keep that man away from Daphne, but he hunts her down. He's her weakness," Mrs. Daniels said.

But Mrs. Daniels' words were just noise to Trisha. She knew chances were that the baby, if Pie was right, had to be Jordan's. Mostly, her hunch was based on how her luck had been running. Trisha thought she should call Jordan and invite him over to share the grim mood. Maybe he could find humor in what a mess his taste in women had made of everything.

Finally, it was time to leave. After seeing Mrs. Daniels to her bed, Pie and Lady Bell came downstairs, gesturing for Trisha to follow. They looked remarkably well for women who had been doing major consoling for hours. Mr. Daniels, looking more pallid, if that was possible, was smashed. They tried to stop him, but he escorted them to the door, stumbling and muttering.

"Thank you, ladies, for your help. Denise is much better," he said with some gratitude. "I'm off to the pharmacy for something for her nerves."

When he was still in earshot, Pie said in a loud voice, "She don't need no tranquilizers. She needs to pray."

Mr. Daniels smiled and shrugged like Pie was joking.

Trisha was to follow them home, the general idea being that Mr. Bell would have less to say about having to make his own dinner if they made an entrance together, but Trisha abandoned the plan, exited at Carrillo. and drove east to Milpas. The Old Spanish Days Parade had passed hours ago, but the street was still packed with revelers ready to drink the night away. It was the Fiesta, the day when Santa Barbara celebrated building the Mission or killing the Indians, or it had something to do with the founding of the city, she didn't know which. Relieved to see Jordan's Triumph in the driveway and the open back door, she parked and hurried inside. Jordan and Art sat at opposite ends of a couch watching a football game.

"Hi, Art, Jordan."

Jordan looked pissed.

"I've been calling you all day. I thought we had plans to go to the Fiesta," he said, drily. Art shifted nervously.

"We need to talk," Trisha said.

Art took that as a clue to leave and hurried into the kitchen.

"What's up?"

"It's about Daphne."

Jordan laughed.

"Daphne? What's there to talk about?"

"Jordan, you need to know this . . . . Daphne might be pregnant."

Jordan sat stone still, then he stood up, grinning.

"Well, good for her. I hope she's happy."

Jordan tried to sound nonchalant, but it was obvious he was stunned. He ran his hands together as though he was drywashing them.

"How do you know it's . . ." She didn't have to finish.

Jordan sighed, then his eyes flashed.

"How the hell would you know she's pregnant?"

"Pie told me."

Jordan slumped forward, face in hands.

"And how would Pie know?"

"Pie used to be a midwife back in Florida. She's seen enough pregnancies."

"Has Pie ever been wrong about anything?"

"Not anything important."

Jordan sighed and meandered to the bathroom. He returned a short time later, face glistening with water.

"It can't be mine. I know . . ."

"Did you use something?"

"No, she did. Why wouldn't she?"

"Maybe she wanted to get . . ."

"Pregnant?" Jordan said, almost choking on the word. "It's Frank's baby. That's what he wanted."

"But that's not what she wanted. She doesn't love him. He probably wants her to have a baby to try to keep her close.

Maybe it's money. He wants her for her money. You didn't. She's crazy, but she's not stupid."

"How do you know I didn't want her for her money?"

"Because you're too in love with her."

"It wasn't love. I was just being stupid," Jordan said.

"You love her now, but you can't admit it to yourself."

"No. I wasn't in love. Love isn't like that."

"She hurt you, but that doesn't matter. You loved her and you still love her, and right now she might be pregnant with your baby."

Trisha could see in Jordan's eyes that he was on the edge of tears. She knew the truth about him. He didn't want to think about his feelings for Daphne. Now, though, he had no choice. Daphne wasn't ever going away if she was carrying his baby.

Jordan shrugged in disgust. He pushed by Trisha, muttering about needing to be alone.

Art came into the living room with a six-pack of Dos Equis.

"Where's Jordan? I thought he wanted to watch the game."

Trisha shrugged as she hurriedly pulled her keys from her purse and headed for the door.

"He's somewhere trying to find out if he has a heart."

Art nodded and turned the game on.

Jordan drove, trying to avoid the crowds milling about after the Fiesta Parade, where blondes dress up in Spanish regalia and march down State Street. Already the frat boys and sorority girls were drunk, wandering around looking for more brewskis. Jordan suppressed the desire to run them over and made it to Mission. He drove up the narrow hillside road to Daphne's studio,

199

thinking hard and fast about what he would say when he got there and what he would do if Frank was with her. The money, her money, abstract wealth, suddenly solidified. Isn't that how the white boys do it, marry into a family with money? All that money. What if she wanted to raise the baby in Australia or England? What if she wanted to have nothing to do with him? Then there was the thought that made him almost deliriously sick: the idea of Frank raising his child. He never wanted to be one of those lowlifes that have a child and walk away like it's somebody else's problem. His parents raised him and loved him, and he damn sure would be there for his own kid, no matter what kind of craziness that would bring.

Daphne's apartment was dark but her Volvo was there. The sock of quarters in his pocket felt ridiculous, but it was either that or a knife. A knife probably would provoke Frank to shoot him, but with a sock full of quarters, he'd either make him laugh or Jordan would brain him.

He knocked but got no response, then he noticed the cobwebs running across the door. Nobody had been there in days. Frank probably had spirited her back to New York.

He drove around the city frantically trying to think of where they could be. All Jordan could think to do was to cruise through parking lots of the hotels where he imagined Frank would stay, searching for his car, but he came across far too many late-model black BMWs.

Then he remembered his date with Daphne at the El Encanto and her mentioning how much she liked the bungalows. He did a U-turn on the narrow road above Mission, saw the city lights flash below him, and red-lined it to the El Encanto. He parked by the fountain, and noticed the valets eyeing him as though he might be up to something. He slowed, consciously trying to present a more amiable, acceptable black face. The valets lost interest and looked elsewhere, and Jordan continued on under the arbor trellises toward the cottages. More BMWs and Benzs and whatnots parked right up to the cottage doors; he finally found Frank's BMW, remembering the license plate, "Carpe Diem!". He put his ear to the door of the bungalow nearest to the car. He heard the sound of someone sobbing.

Jordan pounded on the door until Frank answered. "What?" he said, between sobs. Jordan pulled the sock of quarters out of his pocket, ready to brain Frank right then and there.

"Where's Daphne?" Jordan demanded, pushing by him into the dark room. "Where's the lights?"

Frank closed the door, and now they were in almost total darkness. Jordan could barely see, and Frank was behind him somewhere.

A whimper? At first Jordan thought it was Frank, but no; it was a woman. He heard Frank cursing behind him, and that chased the anger out of Jordan. He frantically searched until he found a wall and ran his hands along it until he found a switch, clicked it on, and saw the wreck of the cottage room. The kicked-over television, the couch on its side, the shattered lamps. On the bed was Daphne, naked, on her stomach, arms outstretched as though she had been trying to hold onto the edges of the bed. Red welts tattooed her back, crisscrossing like a lattice-crust pie.

"I'm sorry," Frank said, almost choking on the words.

"She wanted to leave me. She said she'd file the papers. . . . I never hit . . . hit her before."

Frank stepped back, jerking his hands through thinning hair. It was the first time Jordan took a look at Frank, and he was an ugly sight, shirtless and sunburned, big gut hanging over ridiculously tight Speedos, but his arms were thickly muscled, and he was good at beating somebody down with them.

Jordan approached Daphne and took her wrist.

"Daphne?" he said, and reached to touch her. She gasped at the sound of his voice. He tried to lift her from the bed, but instead he was rocked, smashed against the wall of the bungalow.

"No! Stay away. Leave her alone," Frank shouted.

Jordan found his feet and stood as Frank assumed a guard dog position above Daphne.

"She has to go to the hospital," Jordan said. "What did you do, beat her with a belt or an extension cord?"

"No, you get out!"

Jordan could hear Daphne moaning. She lifted her head, revealing her battered face.

Jordan's shock agitated Frank. His thick arms clapped repeatedly against his chest like a mountain gorilla.

"It's your fault! You poisoned her mind against me. You forced my hand. Fucking nigger!"

"Fuck you!" Jordan shouted, and swung the sock of quarters.

The arcing black band distracted Frank enough so that he stopped to watch the fist-size ball of quarters strike against the side of his head.

He grunted and fell to one knee.

"Good one," he said, and charged again. This time Jordan swung and caught Frank with a blow across the jaw. He sprawled backward, flipping over the upside-down couch.

He saw Daphne attempting to sit up; she hardly had the strength. Jordan wrapped her in a blanket and carried her to the door.

"Thank you," she said, in a whisper.

Outside, his stomach sunk to see the flashing reds and blues rolling up the road.

"What's going on here?" the first policeman asked, stepping from the car.

"Yes, Officer. I came to visit and . . ."

"I want you to put her down and put your hands above your head and kneel down, now!"

"But I'm the one . . ."

"Do it!"

Jordan squatted low and laid Daphne onto the grass as gently as he could manage. He knew without looking that she was unconscious.

"Now, step away from her, turn around, and kneel."

Guns were aimed at him. Reluctantly, Jordan knelt.

The first cop rushed over and handcuffed him, and pulled him over to the patrol car. The cop pushed him inside the backseat and shut the door.

Finally, the ambulance arrived.

"Say, Mort! We've got another one, busted up pretty good."

The two cops led Frank from the bungalow. He had lost the sway in his walk. He now looked calm, together, and most disturbing, he was not handcuffed.

"That's the bastard!" he said, pointing to Jordan.

Jordan was so much in the shit he found it almost funny. Frank strained to get at him, then sobbing, fell into the arms of the cops. Frank was fucking Robert De Niro.

The paramedics went about the job of stabilizing Daphne and strapping her onto the gurney and were gone within minutes, sirens blaring as they drove to Cottage Hospital.

The first cop returned, opened the car door, pulled out a small card, and began reading Jordan his rights.

Jordan couldn't bring himself to respond. Whatever had held his emotions back earlier was gone. Tears flowed from his eyes.

It took a weekend of sharing a tiny cell with a brain-damaged white Rasta busted for ganja possession who taught Jordan the words to "No Woman, No Cry" before Lady Bell, Pie, and Trisha finally sprung him early Monday morning. After the clerk finished the paperwork, Jordan stepped out of custody and approached Trisha sheepishly.

"I don't deserve you, or your friendship," he said, as sincerely as he had said anything in his life.

Trisha sighed and rolled her eyes. Next he hugged Lady Bell and thanked her from the bottom of his heart for bailing him out.

"It wasn't very much," she said, pushing stray bills back into her wallet.

Jordan didn't want to think of how much the bail was. The idea of going to court, getting a lawyer—a lawyer he couldn't afford, to prove his innocence—made him sick to his stomach.

Trisha waited for a quiet moment to speak to him.

"Don't worry, Daphne will explain everything to the police."

Jordan nodded, but he didn't have any confidence she would. He had seen Frank's magic. He could make Daphne sit up and beg.

"I left a message," Trisha said, tentatively. She didn't have to say, it but it was clear; the call wasn't returned. He'd be in the dark until the arraignment.

The lawyer thing was even worse than he had imagined. He would have to go with a public defender, some idiot straight out of law school. But Mr. Bell knew an NAACP attorney who said he'd take the case pro bono. Even though Jordan was grateful, the phone conversation left him sinking lower than he thought he could sink.

205

"Oh, that's a bit of a mess," the lawyer had said, offhandedly.

Jordan's stomach sunk to his knees.

Trisha tried cheering him up but it was hopeless.

"She needed your help. You didn't know what that lunatic was going to do."

"I don't feel very heroic. I feel like I'm going to jail."

"You're not going to jail. Nothing's going to happen to you."

"You sure?" Jordan said, with a smile. "Because I'm not."

"If I just knew what happened," he added.

"Happened with what?"

He looked pained.

"With the pregnancy?" Trisha asked.

"Yeah. Did she lose it?"

Trisha shrugged, and reached for his hand. He realized
then that his relationship with Trisha was the only thing keeping him together.

"I've put you through so much shit."

Trisha smiled.

"I like you a lot, most of the time."

Jordan laughed.

"I don't deserve it."

"Stop being hard on yourself."

"If I had given you what you asked for, none of this mad-
ness would be taking place."

"Given me what?"

"A commitment."

"You've got to want to commit."

"I want to," Jordan said.

"Talk to me when all of this is over. You're so depressed
even marriage looks like a good alternative."

"I'm serious. I think we should get married."

"You'll always love Daphne more than me. You won't say
but you know I'm right," Trisha said.

"You'll see," Jordan said.

Jordan found the ring at a fancy antique store on East Cota
Street. The saleswoman, a former student of his, not only con-
vinced him it was fourteen-karat gold but that the diamond
was real and worth far more than it was priced.

"Oh, yeah. I want it for myself but my boyfriend has a
problem with commitment."

Jordan laughed.

"Tell him commitment isn't jail time. Jail time is jail time."

She looked a little confused at his remark, but just then the phone rang. Jordan looked at the ring again while she was away. He wanted to buy it, but he couldn't afford fifteen hundred; that would take almost all of his savings.

"I can't afford it."

She smiled slyly.

"For his best customers my boss extends credit."

"I'm not one of his best customers."

"Hundred down and a hundred a month until you pay it off."

He nodded and wrote the check.

"I'm just glad to be able to help out a cool teacher," she said.

He watched the pretty girl wrap the ring and it felt very right to him; more right than anything had felt in a long time.

Jordan stopped at the house and showed it to Art.

"It's beautiful, man, nice workmanship. Looks expensive. How much?"

Jordan told him.

"It's a steal. Bet it was part of an estate sale. Trisha's gonna be real happy."

Art nudged him, smiling lasciviously.

"Man, I forgot this," Art said, and handed Jordan a scrap of paper.

"The lawyer called."

Jordan's stomach soured as he glanced at the number. He dialed the lawyer's office.

"Oakley Hall here. A Mrs. Daniels called. She's trying to get in touch with you. Her daughter finally made a statement. You're in the clear. Things are looking good."

Jordan thanked him and hung up, relieved. He immediately drove to Hope Ranch.

Jordan rang the bell, then knocked for a solid minute before he saw Daphne's father coming to answer the door.

"Hello," he said, and looked at Jordan like he didn't know him.

"May I speak to Daphne?"

"Oh, let me find Mrs. Daniels," he said, leaving Jordan at the door.

More movement on the stairs. Daphne! No, Mrs. Daniels.

"Jordan, good to see you. Please come in."

She led him to the couch in the jungle-theme room and gestured for him to sit down. Then she hurried away and returned with two glasses of wine and handed him one.

"I know how hard this must be for you."

"It's been hard."

"As soon as Daphne was in the clear, we had her draft a statement. After hearing how long you had to spend in that jail cell . . . we can never make it up to you."

Pained, she reached over and squeezed his hand.

"We truly appreciate how much you done for Daphne. You were wonderful."

Jordan shrugged awkwardly.

"I really would like to speak to Daphne," he said, but he could already tell it was impossible.

"She's not in the country. She's with her brother in India."

Another long moment. Mrs. Daniels reached for an envelope on the coffee table and handed it to him. Jordan suppressed the desire to tear the letter open because it was obvious Mrs. Daniels wanted him to wait.

"I believe the letter will explain everything."

Jordan stood to leave.

"And there's one other thing," Mrs. Daniels said, and handed him a second envelope. He opened it and took out a multipage document.

"It's a deed for Daphne's apartment on the Riviera."

"A deed?"

"Yes, Daphne owns it. Her grandfather left her that."

"Oh," Jordan said, feeling light-headed.

"She wants you to have it."

209

"What, the property?"

"Yes, for what you went through."

Jordan walked over to the coffee table and retrieved the glass of wine he hadn't touched. He drank it in a gulp.

"You just need to sign it, and I'll have my lawyer file it and the property will be yours."

"What would I do with it?"

"Whatever you like. Sell it, or live there; Daphne loved the place but now she says Frank ruined it for her."

Jordan shrugged, and ignoring the pen Mrs. Daniels held out in front of him, he reached for the pen in his pocket that turned out to be a pencil. Then he saw the pen that Mrs. Daniels had offered him, and signed his name slowly, like a child would, thinking immediately about how much the small property with a view of both the mountains and the ocean must be worth; at least a couple hundred thousand.

He shook Mrs. Daniels' hand, thanked her, and rushed

outside into the brightness of a Santa Barbara morning. He now had his stake in the city; something he had wanted so badly for so long, but now it felt like some stupid, fucking trick, a dumb-ass consolation prize that left him feeling stupid and used. He sat in the car thinking it over, wanting to rush back and demand that deed, to cross his name out, rip it up. But he didn't have that in him.

It came clear to him: Daphne knew what she wanted, and she had it; freedom from Frank, and her own future raising a child. She knew what Jordan wanted too, and she gave it to him.

Finally, Jordan drove away, but he took the northbound 101 and exited at Ellwood Beach. There, he parked at the end of the rows of apartments and walked along the path through groves of eucalyptus trees, to the ocean. He sat down on a bit of path that had survived El Niño, jutting precariously above the sea.

He allowed himself to feel it—the bitterness, the hurt, how much he had loved Daphne, and now what that love had resulted in. He reached into his pocket and tore the letter open. The letter was quite short and typed on something like tissue paper.

Jordan,

Sorry for all the trouble I've caused you. Please do not worry about me. I will write to you as soon as I'm settled in India. Frank is in jail and will be for a long time. I do not plan to return to the States anytime in the foreseeable future. I am due in six months and after that joyous day I

will give you further details. Until then, please
understand how important it is for me to be on my own
and out of contact.

Thank you for giving me the strength to escape my
life.

Love,

Daphne

Below the letter she had scrawled in bright green ink:

Please thank Trisha and her family. They were true
guardian angels. I hope you find the same joy in my little
flat that it gave me.

211

Jordan laughed as he crumpled the flimsy paper. He tried to
sort through the feelings whipping through him, but he couldn't.
Daphne was a calculus that was so beyond him that he didn't
know how to think about it.

It didn't take long for Jordan to reach Trisha's, but he was surprised to see her at the bottom of the driveway.

"Hey, hop in." he said, flinging the door of the Triumph
open.

"I need to bring my father the mail."

"Later! Come on. I've got news."

"What? Did you hear from Daphne?"

He gestured for her to hurry. She gave in and slipped into
the sports car. Jordan sped down the hillside until he reached
the 101 North. When they were miles from Santa Barbara, be-

yond Ellwood Beach and rolling to Santa Ynez, he broke the silence.

"I have a surprise for you and one present."

Trisha smiled warily.

"What?"

"Here," he said, and handed the ring box to her. She opened it slowly as though it were a trick.

"Jordan! You can't afford this. You don't have a job."

"That's the other surprise. I came into some money. My uncle left me something."

"And, it's so much you can afford . . ."

"It's that much. I just have to sell some property."

"Wow."

"And the other news I have for you is . . . I want to pay for your first year of law school."

"You? Pie beat you to it."

"I suppose we can get into married-student housing. That would save a bundle."

After a long awkward moment, Trisha finally spoke.

"Are you saying you want to marry me?"

"Yes, I want to marry you, but I know I fucked up here. I could see how you might not want to be with a guy who gets into the kind of stupid trouble I do."

"Shut up, Jordan. Don't run yourself down. You didn't know that she had her own agenda."

Jordan shrugged and slowed the car, turning off onto an exit that led down a steep decline almost to the ocean's edge. Then he handed Trisha the letter. She read it, shaking her head.

"She's just trying to make herself feel less guilty. If you

212

keep the property, maybe it'll work. There's nothing else to do except to wait and see."

Jordan shook his head despairingly.

"I guess I really cheered you up. Come on. Let's walk to the water," she said.

A few boys played around a beached boat, throwing sand and seaweed at the half-buried hull. Farther up, a sunburned man tossed a Frisbee far out into the surf for his dog to chase.

Jordan's and Trisha's late afternoon shadows stretched ten feet ahead of them as they walked.

"Did you try on the ring?" he asked.

"No, I . . ."

Trisha searched for the ring with growing panic, patting herself down and then Jordan.

"We'll find it," he said. "I have a flashlight."

"Just look," she said, harshly. Trisha found the box wedged into the small space between the Triumph seat and door. Even though the ring was a little tight, she worked it on, smiling happily.

"Never thought I'd see the day," he said.

"I never had a doubt," she said.